"I know it's hard, Serena, but try to stay positive. We will find Petey."

Colt's caring concern brought tears to her eyes, and she leaned against him, desperately needing his comforting voice and arms.

She slid her hands up his torso and rubbed slow circles across his chest. His breath hitched slightly, and he wrapped his arms around her and cradled her against him.

"I just want my son back," she whispered.

"I know, and we will get him back." He pressed a gentle kiss on her forehead and the tears began to slip down her cheeks. But he didn't push for more. Instead, he held her and let her vent her emotions until she finally sighed and wiped at her face.

Then she tilted her head back and looked into his eyes. He'd driven all night and looked tired, but compassion and concern and other emotions she didn't understand registered on his face, as if fatigue never slowed him down. With one thumb, he swept her hair away from her forehead. His lips parted, the whisper of his breath brushed her face.

"Serena?"

"Please kiss me, Colt. Make the pain go away for a while."

RITA HERRON

HER STOLEN SON

TORONTO NEW YORK LONDON
AMSTERDAM PARIS SYDNEY HAMBURG
STOCKHOLM ATHENS TOKYO MILAN MADRID
PRAGUE WARSAW BUDAPEST AUCKLAND

To Billie Jo Case: friend, reviewer, fan…

Recycling programs
for this product may
not exist in your area.

ISBN-13: 978-0-373-69557-7

HER STOLEN SON

Copyright © 2011 by Rita B. Herron

ABOUT THE AUTHOR

Award-winning author Rita Herron wrote her first book when she was twelve, but didn't think *real* people grew up to be writers. Now she writes so she doesn't have to get a *real* job. A former kindergarten teacher and workshop leader, she traded her storytelling to kids for romance, and now she writes romantic comedies and romantic suspense. She lives in Georgia with her own romance hero and three kids. She loves to hear from readers, so please write her at P.O. Box 921225, Norcross, GA 30092-1225, or visit her website at www.ritaherron.com.

Books by Rita Herron

*Nighthawk Island
**Guardian Angel Investigations
†Guardian Angel Investigations: Lost and Found

CAST OF CHARACTERS

Serena Stover—She thought losing her husband was bad, but now someone has framed her for murder and kidnapped her son. The only person who believes her is the handsome detective Colt Mason; but she can't lose her heart again....

Detective Colt Mason—He is determined to save Serena's son, and will do anything to track down the culprit, even if it means exposing her dead husband's dirty little secrets.

Parker Stover—Serena's husband was an undercover agent working on a drug bust. Was he dirty, or had he stumbled on a bigger case that got him killed?

Petey Stover—All Petey wants is to go home and have his family back. But his kidnapper is not out for ransom money—so what does he want with Petey?

Lyle Rice—Serena finally accepted a date with the man, but now she is accused of his murder. Is he really dead or is his murder an elaborate ruse to disguise his real motives?

James Ladden—The ex-con was one of Rice's cellmates; did he abduct Petey?

Detective Geoff Harbison—Parker's former partner left the force shortly after Parker's murder. Was it coincidence or does Harbison have secrets of his own?

Dasha Miller—Serena believes this street girl had an affair with her husband. Does Dasha know the real truth behind her husband's murder and who kidnapped her son?

Hogan Rouse—The hit man who killed Parker claims he murdered the man for money, and may hold the key to Petey's abduction. But the tough, cold prisoner is not talking....

Chapter One

"Mister, will you get my mommy out of jail?"

Colt Mason glanced up from his desk at Guardian Angel Investigations and stared at the dark-haired little boy, surprised at his request.

He was probably what, five or six years old?

"I don't gots a lot of money," the boy said, then hoisted the piggy bank he held in his arms onto Colt's desk. The change inside clanged and rattled as he shoved it toward Colt. "But you can have it all if you'll help me."

Colt grimaced. The last thing he wanted was the boy's savings.

Besides, the kid's eyes were red and swollen from crying, and he was breathing hard as if he'd been running.

Where had he been running from?

"Why don't you sit down, son, and let me get you some water. Then you can tell me who you are and what's going on."

The boy slid into a chair, his shoulders hunched. Colt

stepped from his office into the kitchen, grabbed a bottle of water, brought it back and handed it to him.

The kid's big brown eyes studied Colt warily, but he took the water, unscrewed the lid then took a long drink. Finally he wiped his mouth with the back of his hand and sighed. "My name is Petey Stover. My mommy said people here help kids. And she's in trouble so I come here." Petey pointed to the nameplate on Colt's desk. "You gots the name of a gun."

"Yeah, I do." Colt fought a small smile. "Now, tell me what happened, Petey. How did your mother end up in jail?"

Worry tightened Petey's bowlike mouth. "Last night my mommy had a date with this man named Mr. Lyle. But he pushed Mommy against the fireplace, and then he grabbed her neck." Petey gulped and Colt noticed his hands shake. "I didn't like him hurting her."

Cole clenched his jaw. "I wouldn't like that either. What happened next?"

"She stomped on his foot and kicked him in the… you know—" he pointed to his private parts "—where it hurts."

Colt barely resisted a smile. "Yes, I know. Then what?"

"I tried to pull him away 'cause now Daddy's gone I'm the man of the house." Another deep breath and he squared his small shoulders as if to prove he was a man. "But he knocked me down on the floor."

Anger made Colt grip the chair edge. "He hit you?"

Petey nodded. "Then my mommy got the fire poker and yelled at him to leave."

Colt narrowed his eyes. "Did your mother hit him with the fire poker?"

"No." Petey took another swig of water. "She acted like she would though 'cause she was scared. Then the man got mad and said she'd be sorry."

Colt wouldn't have blamed the woman if she had killed the bastard. "What did he do then?"

"He gives her a mean look but he left." Petey sighed. "So Mommy and I wents to bed. But this morning when I was eatin' cereal, the sheriff came and he said Mommy killed that mean Mr. Lyle, and they taked Mommy away. And this lady with big orange hair took me to kid jail."

Colt's head was reeling. "Kid jail?"

Petey pointed toward the door. "To that big spooky house down the street."

Ah, Magnolia Manor, the orphanage. DFAC had obviously gotten involved.

"But I runned away when they went in for lunch, cause I don't wanna stay in jail, and Mommy shouldn't be there either." He squared his little shoulders. "Jail is for bad people, and my mommy is good. She didn't kill nobody."

Colt took a moment to process the situation. "Where's your father, Petey?"

Petey looked down at his hands where they clenched the water bottle. "He was a policeman, but he got shot and he died."

Poor boy. And now his mother had been arrested.

Petey's chin quivered as he looked back up at Colt. "Will you get her out, Mr. Colt?"

Colt stood. He didn't know if the woman was innocent or guilty but he wanted more details on the matter. "Let me talk to her and we'll see."

Petey jumped off the chair. "Then let's go."

Colt knelt beside the boy. He wasn't a babysitter. Hell, he didn't know much about kids at all.

In fact, he'd screwed up bad when he'd been left in charge of his own brother....

But how could he refuse this little boy? "Petey, I'm sorry, bud, but the sheriff won't allow children in the jail. One of my friends will stay with you here while I talk to your mom. All right?"

"You won't send me back to kid jail?" Petey touched his arm, his voice pleading.

Colt winced. Petey's hands were tiny, just like the rest of him. Yet he had the weight of the world on his shoulders.

He'd been fifteen when he'd lost his own dad and he'd felt that weight on his shoulders. A few months later, he'd failed and lost his brother, too.

Petey was nowhere near that age. Still, he couldn't lie to the child. He would have to call Magnolia Manor sooner or later. "Let me talk to your mom and then we'll make a plan."

Petey nodded, his trusting acceptance sending a streak of guilt through Colt. Still, he went to get Derrick. Derrick could phone Brianna at the manor and smooth things over. She must be frantic.

He hurried to Gage's office, pausing at Derrick's to ask him to join them.

"What's going on?" Gage asked.

"This little boy just came into my office asking for my help. His name is Petey Stover."

Gage switched on the TV in the corner. "His mother was arrested. It's all over the news."

Colt watched as the special news story aired.

"This morning, Serena Stover, wife of former police officer Parker Stover of the Raleigh Police Department, was arrested for the murder of a man named Lyle Rice. Rice was supposedly killed at his home, but police have yet to recover the body. However, evidence quickly led the sheriff to Serena Stover's door."

The camera zeroed in on Sheriff Gray handcuffing and escorting an attractive woman with long, curly, copper-colored hair from her home. She was arguing and protesting, trying to break free to reach her little boy.

Petey was crying and kicking and shouting, determined to wrestle away from the deputy who was hauling him toward another vehicle. A woman Colt assumed to be the social worker was trying to soothe the boy, to no avail.

The camera panned back to Serena as the sheriff pushed her into the back of his squad car. Tears streaked her big eyes as she turned and watched her son beating on the window, screaming her name.

Colt's gut clenched.

"As you can see," the reporter continued, "the arrest quickly became an emotional scene. However, the sheriff feels he has sufficient evidence and motive to move forward."

The camera panned back inside to focus on the crime scene. Massive amounts of blood stained the bedroom floor, and the sheets were blood splattered, one corner dragging the floor. A crime scene tech lifted the corner to reveal more blood.

In fact, Serena's name had been spelled in blood on the wood floor.

"Police believe that Rice scribbled his killer's name in his own blood before he died," the news reporter continued. "More on this story as it develops..."

"That's not good," Gage said.

"If Serena killed Rice and got rid of the body, why wouldn't she have cleaned up?" Colt asked with a frown. "Besides, she sure as hell wouldn't have left her name there for the police to finger her."

"Maybe she was in a hurry and didn't see it," Gage suggested. "The name was covered by the sheet."

Colt shrugged, questions nagging at him.

"Petey was taken to Magnolia Manor, Derrick," Colt said. "Will you let Brianna know he's here and safe?"

Derrick nodded. "She's probably frantic. I'll call her right now." Derrick stepped from the office to make the call.

Gage drummed his fingers on the desk. "This isn't our usual kind of case."

"I know," Colt said. But something about the poor kid and that emotional scene had gotten to him. "The boy is so upset, though. And his story made sense. I'd like to at least talk to the woman."

Gage hesitated, then gave a nod. "All right. But be careful. And don't make an enemy of the sheriff. So far, he's cooperated with us on other cases. I'd like to keep it that way."

Colt agreed and headed back to Petey. He'd be civil to Sheriff Gray, but if he thought the man was wrong about Serena, he wouldn't hesitate to rattle some cages.

There was no way he'd sit by and let him railroad a single mother away from her child if she was innocent.

SERENA STARED at the ink on her fingertips, still stunned that she had been arrested, fingerprinted and was locked in a cell.

Not that it was the first time. But she'd thought her juvenile record was sealed.

She had to get out. The first chance she had, she'd make a break for it. Then she'd find Petey and get him and run.

What kind of life would that be for him, Serena? Hiding out, always making up new names, always afraid...

No, she couldn't do that to her son.

Poor little Petey. He'd been through so much the last two years. His father's murder. Their move to Sanctuary because she'd wanted a nice small town where they could both heal. And they both had started to heal.

Then her friend from work had encouraged her to start dating. A huge mistake.

Lyle Rice had been a charmer at first, then turned

into a snake. When the arrogant animal had pushed Petey, she had wanted to kill him.

But she hadn't, dammit.

And she couldn't run either. She'd given up that life when she'd married Parker. She'd vowed to give Petey a more stable life than she'd had....

Footsteps pounded, the shadow of movement in the hall indicating the sheriff or his deputy had returned. She'd requested her phone call, but the truth was, she didn't even know the name of a good lawyer to call.

Of course, the state would give her a public defender, but she'd had one of those before and that had ended with her in a juvenile facility.

Suddenly the sheriff appeared, along with a broad-shouldered man with hair as black as coal and eyes just as black. He looked powerful, lethal even, with a strong, square jaw and arms that were as big as her legs.

Definitely an alpha guy who was accustomed to being in control. And judging from his short haircut, muscular physique, that laser-intense look and the tattoo on his arm, he was former military.

Either that or a hardened criminal.

Her stomach pitched. Surely, the sheriff wasn't going to lock him in the cell with her.

"Ms. Stover," Sheriff Gray said. "You have a visitor."

Serena crossed her arms, confused. Frightened. Wary.

Who was this man and what did he want with her?

Remembering her husband's horror stories about how

devious police interrogation tactics could be, she braced herself. She had to be careful.

He might be here to trap her into giving a confession.

Chapter Two

Serena adopted a brave face. "Who are you?"

"My name is Colt Mason. I'm a detective with GAI, Guardian Angel Investigations."

Serena frowned, confused even more. "I don't understand. Why do you want to talk to me?"

"It's about your son, Petey," Colt said gruffly.

Serena's mouth went dry, the room swirled around her, and she reached for the bars to steady herself to keep from passing out. Today had been too much, and if something had happened to Petey...

The sound of the cell opening registered, the men murmuring something indiscernible in low voices. Colt gripped her arm and led her to the cot by the wall. Her legs buckled, and she sank onto it, then leaned over, the room spinning in a dizzying circle.

"It's all right. Take a deep breath, Serena," Colt said in a low voice. "Then another."

His soothing tone brought a flood of tears. Angrily she brushed at them and inhaled, determined to regain control. She had to know what had happened to her son. But when she tried to speak, nausea rose to her throat.

The sheriff returned, then Colt pressed a cold cloth against the back of her neck.

Dammit. She needed to be strong. But she'd lost Parker. She couldn't lose Petey. And that blasted woman had promised to take care of him.

Clawing for control, she jerked her head up, removed the cloth from her neck and tossed it aside. Colt Mason was staring at her with those intense black eyes again as if he was trying to see into her mind and soul. Maybe even her heart.

She wouldn't let anyone there, not ever again.

Besides, he was probably trying to judge whether she was a killer.

"Where's my son?" She clutched his shirt. "Is he hurt?"

"Petey is fine," Colt said. "He's at my office."

"What? I thought that social worker took him to a foster home."

Colt covered her hands with his and peeled her fingers loose. "She dropped him off at Magnolia Manor, but as soon as the children went inside for lunch, he bolted and ran down to GAI. Apparently you told him that some nice men there helped children."

Relief mushroomed inside Serena, and she found herself hanging on to his hands. Caution told her not to trust him, but the fact that she had used those exact words with Petey made her relax slightly.

"You have fifteen minutes," Sheriff Gray interjected.

Colt nodded to the sheriff, and he strode back to the front of the jail.

"He must be so scared," she whispered. "Are you sure he's okay?"

"I'm certain." Colt hesitated, an awkward second passing as he released her hands. "Do you feel better now?"

She nodded, searching his strong face for the truth. This man looked hard, cold, forceful, as if he'd seen the worst in humans and was trying to figure out where she stood on the pendulum, if he should be protecting her son from her. That suspicious look cut through her like a knife. "You scared me to death. When you said GAI, I thought…"

"That he'd been kidnapped," Colt said darkly. "I'm sorry. I didn't mean to frighten you. Petey is in my office. One of the other agents, Derrick McKinney, is staying with him. His wife, Brianna, works at Magnolia Manor where the social worker took Petey."

"So you'll send him back there?"

"We have to follow the law, but Brianna is a great lady," Colt said. "She has a son of her own, and loves those kids. Trust me, she'll be like a second mother to him."

He obviously meant to make her feel better, but rage churned through Serena at the thought of anyone else taking care of her son.

"Petey should be with me." She scanned her bleak surroundings. Concrete floor, dingy concrete wall covered in graffiti. Scratchy, faded wool blanket on top of a cot with a mattress so thin the springs bore into her. "And I shouldn't be here. I haven't done anything wrong."

Colt's gaze scrutinized her. "Petey told me a little bit

about what happened," Colt said. "But I'd like to hear your version."

Serena hesitated, doubts creeping in. "Do you have some ID?"

His eyebrow shot up in question, but he removed his wallet and flashed his GAI badge. So he was really a private investigator. "If you're worried that I'm working for the sheriff, I'm not. Your son hired me."

Her gaze latched with his. "Petey hired you?"

A smile quirked at his mouth. "Yes, he offered me all the money in his piggy bank."

Fresh pain and love squeezed her heart. "I'll pay you," she said firmly. "You're not taking Petey's money."

His jaw hardened. "I never said I'd accept it."

She frowned at his curt tone. He almost sounded offended. "It's just that…I feel bad for my son. Ever since my husband died, Petey thinks he has to be man of the house."

A pained look crossed Colt's face. "A big job for a little guy."

"Exactly." Her voice cracked. "He doesn't deserve this right now. He's been through so much already.…"

Colt cleared his throat. "Then let's see if we can clear up this matter, and get you home with him. Now, tell me what happened last night."

Serena chewed on her bottom lip. Lord help her. She hated Parker for dying. And she hated feeling helpless, as if she was failing her son.

Even worse, she hated to give her trust to a stranger. After all, Parker's murder had taught her not to trust anyone.

COLT STUDIED Serena Stover, his nerves on edge. He understood her wariness to trust. If little Petey was telling the truth, it sounded as if Lyle Rice was a bastard and had probably deserved his fate.

But kids lied to protect their mothers all the time. What if she had used that fire poker on the man? Or what if he'd come back after Petey went to bed, and they'd fought? She could argue self-defense.

Unless she had gone after the man with the intent to kill him…

But everything about this woman, from her delicate bone structure to her wild curly hair to those mesmerizing terror-stricken eyes, screamed that she was a victim.

"Serena?" he asked.

She worried her bottom lip for another moment, then inhaled a deep breath. "Like I said before, Petey's father died a couple of years ago. He was a cop, shot in the line of duty."

He didn't know what that had to do with anything, but simply nodded, silently urging her to continue.

"I…haven't dated since he died." She picked at a loose thread on that scraggly blanket. "I didn't want to. I was grieving."

"But you decided to go out with this man Lyle?"

She nodded, regret wrenching her face. "The worst mistake of my life."

He let that comment simmer for a moment. "Go on."

She lifted her gaze to his, tears swimming in the crystal orbs.

God, that hurt look sucker punched him and made him want to yank her in his arms and comfort her. Made him want to promise her he'd make everything right.

But that wasn't a promise he was sure he could keep.

"Serena, I'm not judging you for dating. That's human, normal."

She sighed, then glanced away, and he realized she had judged herself. That she felt guilty, as if she was cheating on her husband when he was dead and never coming back. She must have loved him deeply.

"Anyway, Lyle and I only went out a couple of times," she said softly. "First coffee. Then a movie. But last night we had dinner, and I sensed something was different, that he was ready to take things to the next level."

"You mean sex?"

A blush crept onto her cheeks, then a sliver of fear darkened her eyes. "Yes."

"But you weren't ready?"

She shook her head. "No. Not at all." She swallowed, then licked her lips, making him uncomfortably aware that she was sensuous and fragile and a woman.

"Anyway, when he brought me home, he came in for a drink, which I never should have allowed," she added beneath her breath. "Then he came on to me. I told him right away that it wasn't going to work between us and asked him to leave."

Colt didn't like the images forming in his mind. "But he didn't?"

She twisted that ratty blanket in her hands, fidgeting. "No, he got angry, then pushy. I asked him to leave again, but he refused to accept my rejection, and he pushed me against the fireplace."

She paused, her breath coming faster. "Then Petey came in, and…" Emotion thickened her voice. "Petey tried to pull him away from me, but he threw him to the floor."

Her hands knotted into fists around the blanket. "So I grabbed the fire poker and ordered him to get out."

"Then he left without a fight? You two didn't struggle?"

"No, but I did knee him in the groin. Then he did leave." She ran a hand through her hair. "But he was seething and before he went out the door, he warned me I'd be sorry, that I had no idea who I was messing with."

She dropped her head into her hands. "God, I am sorry, but not that I told him to leave. I'm sorry I ever met the man."

So far her story matched Petey's.

Colt gripped the cot edge to keep from drawing her up against him. Her fragile body was trembling, her lip turning blue where she kept worrying it with her teeth.

"What happened after he left?"

She shifted restlessly, wiping at her tear-stained cheeks. "Petey was upset, so I cuddled him for a while and lay down with him until he fell asleep. This morning we were having breakfast when the sheriff knocked on the door." She waved her hand. "Then they tore Petey away from me and arrested me.…"

"Lyle didn't come back during the night? Maybe he broke in and attacked you—"

"No," Serena said firmly. "He didn't come back, I didn't fight with him, and I didn't go to his place. In fact, I've never been to his house." Her voice grew stronger. "And I would never leave Petey alone. *Never.*"

Colt frowned. "Do you have proof, someone who can alibi you?"

"Petey, but he was asleep."

"Did you make or receive any phone calls during the night? Were you on the computer?"

"No, I fell asleep beside Petey, then woke up around four and went to my bed."

Damn. A typical single mother routine, but not much for an alibi.

Colt tapped his foot, thinking. "Did the sheriff mention the evidence he has against you? How he knew you were involved with Rice?"

Serena's forehead puckered. "No."

"How about the cause or time of death?"

She shook her head. "No, he hasn't told me anything."

A situation he would rectify.

"Tell me more about Rice. What did he do for a living? How did you two meet?"

Serena heaved a breath. "He told me he was an entrepreneur, that he had investments in small companies. I run a bookkeeping business out of my home, and one of my clients gave him my name as a reference in case he needed my services."

He definitely needed more background information on Rice. "Have you phoned a lawyer yet?"

A sense of despair seemed to wash over her. "No. I haven't had a chance to call." Her voice cracked again. "Besides, I don't know *who* to call. I've never needed a criminal attorney before." She swung her gaze toward the cell door. "I can't believe I need one now."

Colt gave up the battle to keep his distance, and tugged her hands into his. "Listen to me, Serena. I know a good lawyer. I'll put in a call to her."

The sheriff's footsteps echoed down the hall, and Colt stood. "Hang in there. I'll call my friend about arranging your bail. And I'm going to question the sheriff and find out more about Rice's murder."

Sheriff Gray appeared at the door, keys jangling as he motioned to Colt.

Serena rose and gripped his arm. "Please, Colt. Tell Petey I love him. And don't let him end up in the system. I grew up there myself. It's not pretty."

He'd been a cop long enough to know what could happen, too. But the law was the law, and his hands were tied.

Petey was going back to Magnolia Manor.

SERENA PACED the jail cell, the tiny space closing around her. The nauseating scent of old sweat, urine and dirt wafted around her, nearly suffocating her.

She felt trapped. Panicky. And worried sick about her son.

Colt Mason's face flashed into her mind, and a sliver of something frightening stirred in her belly. He had a strong, prominent jaw that seemed permanently set in anger. That crooked nose, the scar on his forehead and his black, intense eyes gave him a menacing look.

But she'd heard a tenderness in his voice when he'd mentioned Petey. And if he worked with GAI—and she had seen his badge as proof—then he had to answer to his boss and the other agents, meaning he had to be legitimate.

His questions about Lyle also roused her own questions. What would the sheriff tell him about her case? Sheriff Gray had to have some kind of evidence to hold her. But what kind of evidence could he possibly have against her?

Her shoulders and body ached with fatigue and tension, and she collapsed onto the cot, sick at the thought of having to spend the night in the cell.

At the thought of Petey sleeping in a foster home or orphanage where God knew what could happen to him.

He was so little, so young. He wouldn't know how to protect himself against the bullies or the street-savvy kids. And he didn't have enough strength to protect himself if one of the caretakers assaulted him.

Memories of one foster father in particular taunted her, and she automatically rubbed at the scar below her breastbone.

His wife…she'd been just as bad. A religious fanatic who'd sacrificed Serena to her husband in order to save herself from his vile touches. God's will, the woman had said.

But God never meant for a man to do the things that

man had done to her. God never meant for people to hurt children.

Tears threatened again, but she willed them away and let her mind go to that safe place where she'd retreated as a child. Where nothing could hurt her. Not the evil touches of those who pretended to care for children, not their hateful words or degrading comments or their beatings.

She was not that little girl anymore. She was strong. She had found love once. She had a son, and she would die protecting him.

Suddenly exhausted, she lay back on the cot and closed her eyes. But just as she was about to fall asleep, the image of Lyle Rice's face materialized. Then her foster father.

Except this time he and Lyle were teaming up, and they were both chasing Petey...

She jerked up, shaking all over, a chill skating up her spine.

Please, Colt, help me. And please hurry...

PETEY ROCKED back and forth in the big chair, his legs dangling. Mr. Colt had been gone a long time.

He kept staring at the door, hoping he'd come in any minute.

Hoping his mommy would be with him and she'd take him home. And this horrible day would be over.

Mr. Colt's friend Mr. Derrick set a drawing pad and some crayons on the coffee table. "Wanna draw while we wait on Colt to get back?"

He stared at the crayons and paper for a minute. He

was a pretty good drawer. But he didn't feel like drawing. His stomach was growling and jumping up and down, he was so hungry.

Maybe he should have broken out of jail after that mac and cheese.

Petey shook his head. "No. I wanna go home."

Mr. Derrick nodded. "I know. Maybe when Colt returns, he can tell us when you and your mother can go home."

Footsteps squeaked on the floor. His heart pounded. He sat up straighter. His mommy was coming back now. She'd hug him hard, and then they'd get lunch and ice cream and forget about this awful day.

But Ms. Brianna walked in the door instead.

Petey went stone-cold still.

Mr. Colt hadn't helped him at all. He'd lied to him.

Tears clogged his throat. He'd trusted him 'cause his name was the name of the gun his daddy had told him about.

But Mr. Colt had called the kid jail to come and get him.

Would they put those metal things on his hands this time like they had his mommy to keep him from running away again?

Chapter Three

Serena's comment about being in the system disturbed Colt. What had happened to her while she was in foster care? Had someone hurt her?

Knowing that was very possible, he hated even more that her son would be forced to stay in the orphanage or with a foster family until this mess was sorted out and she was cleared.

Granted she *was* cleared.

God knew he'd seen enough cases go awry not to completely trust the court system.

Colt stepped into the front office and phoned Kay Krantz, an attorney he'd met when he was on the force. She was kind, compassionate and a pit bull in court. As soon as he explained that Serena was a single mother whose husband had been killed on the force, she agreed to rush over.

Next he phoned Ben Camp at GAI. Ben was their go-to technical guy. If he couldn't hack into it or trace it, it couldn't be done. "Ben, it's Colt. Did you talk to Derrick?"

"Yeah, he filled Gage and all the agents in on your case. Where are you?"

"The sheriff's department. I just met with the little boy's mother, and I believe her story." He explained about Lyle Rice's advances, Serena's rejection and that the man had hurt the boy.

"How was he killed?"

"I don't know any details yet, but I'm going to talk to the sheriff now. I also phoned Kay Krantz, and she agreed to represent Serena. She's on the way."

"So you believe this Stover woman is innocent?"

Colt hesitated. He'd been fooled by women before. But not for a long time. One plus of working undercover was that he'd become a good judge of character, both good and bad. "Yeah, I do."

"Then I'll see what I can dig up on Rice. If the man has skeletons, they're coming out of the closet."

"Thanks, Camp. I'll update you once I talk to Sheriff Gray."

Colt strode to the sheriff's office and knocked on the door. The sheriff glanced up from the file on his desk and gestured for him to come in.

"I didn't expect to have GAI in on this investigation," Sheriff Gray said without preamble.

Colt shrugged. "Her kid made a good case."

Gray nodded, his expression troubled. "I haven't interrogated Ms. Stover yet. She was too upset when we first brought her in."

So the sheriff had a touch of compassion. If he'd really believed the woman was a cold-blooded killer, he would have gone for the jugular before she'd had time to concoct a phony story.

Colt crossed his arms. "So, what evidence do you have against Serena Stover to warrant an arrest?"

Sheriff Gray leaned back in his seat, and propped his feet on his desk. "You know I don't have to tell you that."

"True. But I have a feeling you will."

"Does Ms. Stover have a lawyer?"

Colt folded his arms. "She's on her way."

Sheriff Gray nodded as if he'd expected as much. "Then we might as well discuss it all at once."

Colt wanted answers now. "The news reporter said you didn't find a body. Have you recovered it yet?"

Sheriff Gray fiddled with the pen on his desk. "No."

Colt frowned. "Then how can you be certain there was a murder?"

"There is other convincing evidence," the sheriff said in a tone indicating he didn't intend to argue—or reveal all the information he had at the moment.

"How about cause of death?"

Gray's expression shut down. "I told you we'd discuss this with Ms. Stover and her attorney. Now, I need to make a call."

Colt hesitated. He wanted to push for more, but Sheriff Gray gestured toward the door, and he remembered Gage's warning about staying on Gray's good side.

Anxious for the attorney to arrive, he stepped outside to wait for Kay. But questions nagged at him. What the hell did Gray have on Serena?

Whatever it was, it had to be pretty damn convincing.

A red convertible zoomed down the street, then whirled into a parking spot in front of the sheriff's office. Kay Krantz. A second later, she climbed out, looking all-business in a tailored blue suit. She was a beauty, but it was the ferocious attorney at work that he admired.

Still, there had never been anything between them except friendship and a healthy respect for each other's jobs. Like Serena, she was still grieving over the loss of her husband. Maybe one day she'd move past it and some lucky bastard would snag her.

Right now, he just wanted her to help Serena Stover and her little boy.

"You talked to the sheriff?" she asked, slinging a black leather briefcase over one shoulder.

"He's waiting for you." He opened the door to the sheriff's office, and she sashayed inside. "By the way, he hasn't questioned Serena yet. She was too upset when he arrested her."

Her eyebrow quirked at that, but she flipped a strand of her long black hair over her shoulder and forged on. The moment she entered the office, the sheriff's eyes lit up.

"Kay Krantz," she said, then extended her hand.

Sheriff Gray stood and shook her hand. "You're representing Serena Stover?"

"That's right." Her fingers tightened around the strap of her shoulder bag. "I'd like to see a copy of the arrest warrant."

Frowning, the sheriff snagged it from his desk

and pushed it into her hands. "I can assure you it's in order."

She studied it for a moment, then dropped it on to the desk. "Okay, let me see my client now."

"Fine," Sheriff Gray said. "I'll move her to the interrogation room and we'll all convene there." He glanced at Colt. "You can wait here."

"He's with me," Kay said, then smiled when Gray narrowed his eyes. "My assistant."

"Yeah, right," Gray muttered, then jangled his keys as he went to retrieve Serena.

Five minutes later, they were all seated in the interrogation room. Serena and Kay sat on one side of the table across from the sheriff. Colt parked himself at the end. Gray had already given him orders to keep his mouth shut.

He hoped he could comply, but he wasn't promising anything.

Still, he adopted his poker face, the one he used when he was undercover. Sometimes a person's mannerisms said more than their words. He just hoped that Serena told the truth.

And that she didn't have any ghosts in her past the sheriff could use against her.

SERENA GRIPPED her clammy hands together, bracing herself to be ripped apart by the sheriff's questions.

Kay Krantz squeezed her hand, and she took a deep breath. When the lawyer had introduced herself, Serena remembered the attorney's name from a big case in Raleigh.

Kay Krantz had won.

Hopefully, she was as talented as the article had claimed.

"All right, Sheriff," Kay said. "Show us what you have."

Sheriff Gray's face remained solemn as he opened a folder and spread photos of a ransacked bedroom in front of them. The light was dim, the furniture old and outdated, but it was the mess that caught Serena's eyes. Clothes were scattered in disarray, a lamp was overturned, a wineglass broken on the faded carpet.

Then her gaze fell to the bed, and her stomach pitched. The white bed linens were tangled and drenched in blood.

"We believe Mr. Rice was killed here in his bedroom." Sheriff Gray gestured toward the crimson stains on the sheets and floor. "As you see from the amount of blood loss, he was apparently stabbed several times and bled out."

Serena couldn't take her eyes off the blood. No one could have survived that much blood loss.

Kay gestured toward the other photos of the crime scene. "Then where is Rice's body?"

The sheriff twisted toward Serena, his suspicious look sending a chill up her spine. "We were hoping Ms. Stover could tell us that."

"I have no idea," Serena blurted. "I—"

"Shh, don't say anything right now." Kay placed her hand over Serena's to calm her.

"What about the murder weapon?" Kay asked.

The sheriff pointed to a serrated kitchen knife on the

floor beside the tangled bedding, and cold fear clawed at Serena. Dear God…that knife looked exactly like one from the set Parker's parents had given them as a wedding gift.

"Blood matches Rice's. And we found Ms. Stover's prints on the knife, and the wineglass."

Serena gasped. "But I've never been to the man's house."

Sheriff Gray leaned forward, hands gripping the file edge. He slid another photograph from the bottom of the stack and cocked one brow.

"Then how did your underwear and prints get in his bedroom, Ms. Stover?"

Serena stared at a pair of her black lace underwear in shock. "I have no idea, I told you I've never been in his house…"

The sheriff's look hardened. "Just like you weren't guilty of assault when you were a teenager?"

Serena gasped. "I wasn't. Besides, those records were supposed to be sealed."

Again Kay covered her hand to silence her. "Serena, please. Let me handle this."

Serena gave Colt an imploring look, hoping for support, but his face was a granite mask revealing nothing.

They had to believe her. She hadn't been at Lyle's house.

Of course, she hadn't attacked that guy when she was fifteen either. She had been defending herself. But the boy who'd accosted her came from a rich family who'd paid a high-priced attorney to drag her through the mud, and she'd ended up in the juvenile detention center.

So how *had* her underwear and knife and her fingerprints gotten in Lyle's place?

Sheriff Gray laid another photograph in front of them. "These are from Rice's computer." He spread several printouts of emails in front of her, then used a pencil to point to them. "Please read these emails, Ms. Stover."

Trembling inside, Serena leaned forward to study the screen and Kay did the same.

I love you, Lyle. I won't let you leave me. I'll kill you before I let you go.
You're mine forever.
Serena

Nausea settled over her as she scanned a dozen more. Each note poured out her love, begged the man to not leave her, the latter ones becoming increasingly threatening.

But she hadn't sent them.

"Judging by these emails, it appears you were obsessed with Lyle Rice." The sheriff's chair squeaked as he leaned back, studying her. "Rice wasn't upset because you rejected him, Ms. Stover. It was the other way around. You were stalking him."

"No…that's not true—"

"Be quiet, Serena." Kay's fingers tightened over Serena's. "Sheriff, how do you know those emails came from my client? Did you have a warrant to search her computer?"

Sheriff Gray smiled. "I'm not some dumb local like you think, Ms. Krantz." He lifted a manila envelope from a file box and dropped it on the desk, then removed Serena's cell phone, which was sealed in a plastic bag.

"When we booked Ms. Stover, we collected her personal items. The emails came from this phone."

Serena's heart pounded. "That's impossible."

"Someone else could have used that phone to plant those emails," Kay pointed out calmly.

Sheriff Gray shrugged, then angled his head toward Serena. "But you sent them, didn't you, Ms. Stover? You were desperate for attention after your husband's death, so you fell for the first man who came along. Then you couldn't stand it when Rice broke it off with you, so you stalked him, then went to his house and stabbed him." Sheriff Gray's voice hardened. "Now tell us where you dumped the body, and maybe we can talk a plea."

"There's no need to discuss a plea. My client is innocent." Kay glared at the sheriff in challenge. "Sheriff, look at Ms. Stover. She can't weigh more than one hundred and ten pounds. Rice was much larger and stronger, right?" She glanced at Serena. "How much did he weigh? One-eighty, two-hundred pounds?"

Serena nodded.

"First of all, it would be highly unlikely that Serena could overcome a man that size and stab him. Secondly, if she did, he would have put up a fight and she would have major defensive wounds." Kay ticked her points off on her fingers. "And thirdly, even if she overcame those obvious obstacles and managed to kill him, how could she have possibly gotten rid of the body by herself?"

Sheriff Gray punched the first photograph of the crime scene. "See those marks on the floor? There used to be a rug in that spot. She used it to roll up the man's body." He slanted Serena a condemning look. "Then you dragged him outside, put him in your van and dumped him somewhere. Where? A ravine maybe? The river?"

Kay rolled her eyes. "There is no way my client could have lifted Rice into her van by herself."

Sheriff Gray tilted his head sideways. "You'd be surprised at how strong an adrenaline rush can make a person."

Kay shot up from her seat, her tone sarcastic. "Sheriff, this is ridiculous. The next thing you're going to accuse her of is having an accomplice. Maybe her six-year-old son helped her dump the body."

"Why don't you let your client tell us how she disposed of Rice's body?" Sheriff Gray suggested.

Serena glared at him, biting back an argument. At this point, shouting and arguing would only make her look guilty. As if his evidence hadn't already done that.

"As I said, my client is innocent, Sheriff." Kay reached for her briefcase. "Now this interrogation is over. I demand you release Ms. Stover."

"We'll let the judge decide that in the morning," Sheriff Gray said.

"But you have no case." Kay glared at him. "You don't have a body so you have no definitive proof of a crime, especially a murder. And all your evidence is circumstantial."

"It may be circumstantial," Sheriff Gray said. "But it

is enough to hold your client, and enough to convict her. And for your information, I have a warrant to confiscate Ms. Stover's vehicle and have it searched and processed for evidence." He checked his watch. "In fact, it's probably being confiscated as we speak."

Pure panic seized Serena. She wanted to deny that he would find anything incriminating in her van. But already he had evidence that boggled her mind. Evidence that had to have been planted.

But who would frame her for murder?

Dear God. If she was convicted, Petey would definitely go to foster care. She couldn't lose him or spend the rest of her life in jail for a crime she hadn't committed.

"Ms. Stover, do you have anything to say?" the sheriff asked.

Serena glanced at Colt. He was watching her with hooded eyes. Judging her. Trying to decide whether or not he believed her.

For some reason, that hurt more than the sheriff's blatant accusations.

She straightened, injecting sincerity into her voice. "Just that I am innocent. I did not kill Lyle Rice, I swear it."

The sheriff stood then as if dismissing them. "Ms. Krantz, your client's bail hearing is set for ten in the morning. We'll see you then."

Kay's eyes darkened with anger, but she nodded, then turned to Serena. "Hang in there, Serena. We'll get you out of here as soon as possible."

"But what about my son?" Serena clenched her

hands into fists. Maybe she should have stolen those keys, snagged Petey and run. "Petey's scared. He needs me."

"You should have thought about that before you killed Rice," Sheriff Gray mumbled.

"That's enough, Sheriff." Colt stepped toward the sheriff. "While you're wasting time bullying an innocent single mother, the real killer, if there *was* indeed a murder, is free and escaping right now."

Sheriff Gray glared at him then clutched Serena's arm and hauled her toward the door.

COLT HATED like hell to leave Serena in jail for the night. Gray was being a hardass. Dammit, Serena's juvenile record didn't help.

He had to find out the story behind that arrest.

Still, he hoped Gray didn't toss another prisoner in the cell with Serena, especially one who might be violent.

Petey's face flashed in his mind. Her son would have to spend the night at Magnolia Manor.

He didn't like it, but his hands were tied. And finding Rice's killer—or his body if he was still alive—was the best way he could clear Serena and reunite her with her son.

Circumstantial or not, the evidence Gray had was pretty damn convincing.

You have been fooled before, he reminded himself. *And nearly died for it.*

Only this time he would be smarter. This time he

wouldn't become personally involved. Wouldn't get close to Serena or her son.

But he would finish the case. The fact that the evidence was circumstantial and there was no body threw up red flags. He didn't peg Serena for the stalker type either.

Of course, there was her prior record....

That was years ago, though, and she'd said she'd grown up in the system. He needed to hear the whole story before he gave credence to that arrest.

For now, he'd talk with some of her employers, friends and neighbors and find out what the adult Serena was like. He didn't believe for a minute that Serena had left her son alone, driven to Rice's house, murdered him, dragged him to her van and dumped his body.

Not that little bitty woman who adored her son and was sick over the idea of him being in foster care.

Trying to deflect images of her alone in that ugly cell sleeping on that nasty cot—or not sleeping, most likely—he climbed in his Range Rover and drove back to GAI. He had to update the team, see what Ben had found, and start questioning everyone who knew Serena to establish her character references.

They also needed to canvas Rice's neighborhood for witnesses. Maybe someone spotted another vehicle the night before or heard an altercation that might lead them to the truth.

Late afternoon shadows obliterated the sun as it slipped behind the horizon, and his gut tightened. It would be a long night for Serena.

And for Petey.

Steeling himself as he parked, he strode inside. He paused at his office, but it was empty so he strode to Derrick's. Brianna's voice echoed from inside, then he heard baby Ryan babbling.

As he turned the corner, he spotted Petey slumped on the couch watching the baby, his little face riddled with worry. Derrick glanced up as he entered, and so did Petey.

Petey's face fell. "I thought you was bringing my mommy back."

Colt swallowed against the knot in his throat, then stooped in front of Petey. "I just came from seeing her, bud, and she's okay. But it'll be tomorrow before she's released."

"No!" Petey jumped up and bunched his hands into fists. "No, she gots to come get me so we can go home and make hot dogs and read stories and play with my action figures." He heaved for a breath, a sob escaping at the end.

"I'm sorry, Petey," Colt said. "I did everything I could. But the judge won't see us until morning. Then we'll post bail and your mommy can come home."

"But I wants her tonight," Petey wailed.

"Petey," Brianna said softly. "Remember what I told you about Magnolia Manor? It's not a bad place. The kids are nice, and they'll play with you, and Ms. Rosalie will read you stories."

Petey slammed his fist into Colt's chest. "No, you lied. You're sending me back to kid jail. I don't wanna go to jail!"

Colt's gut clenched, but he let the little boy purge his

anger, accepting his blows until Petey finally collapsed against him in a sobbing fit.

Brianna and Derrick both watched with sympathetic looks. Baby Ryan even stopped playing to look up at Petey, his lip quivering as if he might burst into tears, as well.

"Colt," Derrick said. "Instead of sending Petey back to the manor, Bri and I will take him home for the night."

Brianna rubbed Petey's back where he lay against Colt's chest, exhausted and spent. "That's a great idea. Petey, you can spend the night with Ryan."

Colt gave them a grateful look. Brianna was experienced with kids, and much better equipped to deal with an angry, frightened child than he was. "Thanks. I'm sure his mother would appreciate that."

Besides, he couldn't babysit Serena's little boy and investigate her case at the same time. Yet holding Petey stirred some kind of primal instincts that he didn't even know he possessed.

"Petey," he murmured. "You're not going back to the manor right now. Mr. Derrick and Ms. Brianna want you to spend the night with them and baby Ryan."

Petey hiccupped on another sob but didn't respond.

Colt carried him out to Derrick's car, and Petey slumped into the seat, eyes red and swollen. He glared up at Colt as if he hated him.

"I know you're mad at me." Guilt stabbed Colt at Petey's accusatory look. "But you asked me to get your mommy out of jail, and I'm going to do that, Petey. I promise." He leaned forward. "But I need your help.

Your job is to be nice to Ms. Brianna and Ryan. Then Ryan's daddy can help me clear your mom."

Petey's lower lip trembled. "If my daddy was here, he wouldn't have let them take mommy or me away."

Colt gritted his teeth. That might be true. But his dad was gone.

And right now, he was all Petey and Serena had.

Colt reached inside his pocket and withdrew a small shiny whistle. He'd never forgotten the day his father had given it to him. It was the day a police officer had come to school to talk to the children about strangers.

He handed it to Petey. "My father gave this to me when I was about your age. He told me to blow it if I ever needed help. I want you to take it. But remember, only use it if you need it."

Petey's hand trembled as he wrapped his fingers around the whistle.

Then Colt watched Derrick drive away, Petey's face haunting him.

COLT SPENT THE EVENING canvassing the homes near Rice's, but no one seemed to know anything. According to an elderly woman two units down, the man had moved in a month before and kept to himself. Others claimed they'd only seen him coming and going. None had really talked to him.

And no one had heard anything the night before. No cars. No arguments. No screams.

On a positive note, not one of them had seen Serena Stover or her minivan anywhere near the man's house.

So what the hell had happened to Rice?

And who was framing Serena?

A dozen more questions bombarded him as he wolfed down a pizza. He spent a couple of hours online himself researching Rice, but found very little about the man in cyberspace.

Which raised more questions. An entrepreneur involved in several small businesses should have more of a presence on the internet.

He typed in the link to Serena's business and accessed her records, then phoned two of her clients. Both gave her raving character descriptions, claiming she was nice, professional and adored her son. All seemed shocked at her arrest.

He tried a different tactic for Rice, searching for more on his background, and was still digging around for information at 2:00 a.m. when the phone trilled.

Colt frowned and grabbed the handset.

"Colt, it's Derrick." His voice sounded choppy, strained, upset.

"What's wrong?"

"It's Petey. He finally fell asleep around midnight, and then we went to bed, too. But I heard a noise a few minutes ago and got up, and...dammit, Colt."

Colt's heart raced. "What?"

"Petey's gone."

Chapter Four

"Petey's gone?" Colt's heart hammered.

"Yes," Derrick said, his voice strained. "We've searched the house and outside, but we can't find him anywhere."

"Dammit, he could have run away again."

"That's what I thought. I'm going to take the car and comb the neighborhood." Derrick released an explosive breath. "Bri has already called Rosalie at the manor, but I don't think Petey would go back there."

"Me neither." So where would the kid go? "He was furious at me," Colt said. "Maybe he was coming here."

"How would he know where you live, man?"

Colt scrubbed his hand over his face. "Right. That doesn't make sense."

"Maybe he's running toward the jail," Derrick suggested.

Colt contemplated that possibility. "Maybe, but we told him that they won't allow children there." He tried to put himself in the head of a six-year-old. "He'd probably go someplace safe."

"Someplace he felt close to his mother," Derrick murmured.

"His home." Colt grabbed his keys and headed toward the door. "I'll go to Serena's. You check outside and the neighborhood, and I'll call the sheriff and tell him Petey is missing in case he does turn up at the jail."

"Are you going to have him tell Serena?" Derrick asked.

Colt jumped in his Range Rover and started the engine. "No, not yet. She'll be terrified. Let's see if we can find him first before we have to put her through that worry."

Colt disconnected the call, then punched in the sheriff's number. He answered on the third ring. "Sheriff Gray, this is Colt Mason. We have a problem."

"Do you know what time it is?" the sheriff barked.

"Petey Stover is missing."

A tense heartbeat passed. "What the hell happened?"

"He was upset when I didn't bring his mother back. So Derrick McKinney and his wife took him to their house."

"I thought he was in foster care."

"Brianna works for Magnolia Manor. She—we—thought he'd be better off tonight with them. But Derrick just phoned and said the boy is gone. He's searching the neighborhood, but I thought you should check the jail in case he goes there to be with his mother."

Sheriff Gray muttered a sound of frustration. "Deputy Alexander is at the jail now. I'll call him, issue an amber alert and cruise the town."

Colt sighed. "Thanks. I'm going to Serena's in case he goes home."

The men disconnected, and Colt headed toward the Stover house. He just prayed that Petey was there and not out wandering the streets all alone.

SERENA HAD FINALLY fallen asleep, but nightmares haunted her—she was locked away in a hellhole with hardened criminals, with women who called her names and beat her, and guards who used her for their own pleasures.

Jerking awake, she shivered in the cold darkness, the putrid scents of urine and sweat lingering from past prisoners wafting around her as a reminder of the scum who landed in jail.

That she might be one of them if Kay Krantz and Colt Mason didn't find out who had killed Lyle. That her juvenile record might cost her dearly.

"I'm so sorry, Parker," she whispered. She'd promised to take care of their son but she'd failed miserably, all because of her own selfish needs. She'd been lonely and had invited Rice into their lives.

She would never put her own needs ahead of her son's again.

The image of Petey's terror-stricken, tear-stained face pressed against the window as he was torn away from her taunted her. Who was taking care of her son tonight? Had someone read him a story? Made sure he brushed his teeth?

Who had tucked him in bed and tickled his belly and kissed him good-night?

Shaking with renewed anger, she shoved the ratty blanket away, unable to stand the vile smell any longer.

But she was too tired to sit up or do anything but stare at the nasty words carved on the walls.

A spider wove a tangled web in the corner of the cell, and she watched it work, thinking how elaborately the spider planned its trap.

She was the fly caught in the web now.

Because someone had orchestrated an elaborate plan to frame her for Lyle's murder.

Her head hurt from trying to figure out the puzzle. Who had killed Lyle? And why frame *her?*

How could she prove that the evidence the sheriff had against her had been planted?

AS COLT DROVE TOWARD Serena's, he scanned the streets and alleys, hoping to spot Petey. But the darkness made it almost impossible to see, and intensified his worries. The mountains were massive, filled with dangers and places to hide.

Would Petey even know how to find his way from Derrick's house to his own?

What if he was lost? Or what if some driver couldn't see him and accidentally hit the poor kid?

He never should have put Petey in that car. He should have brought him home with him.

He was the one Petey had asked for help, and he had betrayed the boy by allowing the social worker to cart him away, and then by sending him to Derrick's. But he'd honestly thought Petey would feel comfortable with Brianna.

The streets were quiet, and except for an occasional car, traffic was virtually nonexistent. He veered onto Sycamore, keeping his eyes peeled for Petey, but all he spotted was a stray dog wandering through one of the yards. A catfight broke out somewhere behind one of the houses, the shrill screeching unnerving in the night.

A lone light glowed in a room in a neighbor's house, but most of the houses were dark, attesting to the fact that everyone was in bed.

Where Petey belonged.

He eased into Serena's driveway, scanning the property. A nice white little bungalow with a fenced backyard. A porch swing on the front porch and the scooter and football in the yard gave the place a homey feel, another reminder that this house belonged to a single mother and her son.

Ones who'd had their lives uprooted today. The question was, why?

He cut the engine, then moved quietly toward the front door, checking windows and locks. All shut down. The house was shrouded in darkness, as well.

If Petey had come home, would he hide out in the dark like this?

He circled around the side to the back again, checking windows, but they were all locked, and so was the back door. He wanted inside.

But he hated to break a window or lock. Rational thought kicked in, and he pivoted, searching the back patio for a place Serena might have hidden a backup key.

A fort for Petey had been erected in the backyard, a bicycle lay on its side, and flowerpots filled with geraniums and impatiens flanked both sides of the patio.

He stooped and dug beneath the first one but found nothing. Three more pots and his hand closed around the key. Using it to let himself in, he paused to listen for sounds. Any indication that Petey was inside.

The ticktock of a clock somewhere in the house echoed in the silence along with the low hum of the refrigerator and air conditioner.

"Petey, it's Colt."

Not wanting to frighten the kid if he was here, he inched his way inside, then moved slowly across the room and flipped on a light. "Petey, if you're here, please come out. I promise I'm not going to take you back to the manor."

Nothing.

He crept into the den and switched on a lamp, blinking at the sudden brightness. The room was painted a pale yellow with a dark green couch and comfy chairs situated around a fireplace. Children's books and toys occupied one corner. Family photographs decorated a far wall. He paused to study one of Petey and his dad, and his gut tightened. Serena had said her husband was killed in the line of duty.

Old instincts kicked in. Police work was dangerous. Had her husband's killer been arrested? Had his killer decided to come after Serena and Petey for some reason?

If so, could it be related to Rice's murder, and the fact that Serena had been conveniently framed?

He rubbed the back of his neck. Maybe he was making a wild jump, but it might be worth looking into.

He glanced at the room that opened to the right and realized it was Serena's office. A neat desk, filing cabinet, computer.

But no Petey.

Across the other side a small hallway led to two bedrooms. He flipped on a hall light and veered into the first one. The room was painted a warm red with a white comforter and red-and-white striped curtains. Obviously Serena's room. "Petey, are you here, bud? If you are, please come out and talk to me. I want to help you."

The floor squeaked as he knelt and checked under the bed, then he searched the closet and bathroom. All empty.

Damn. One more room.

Petey's. Maybe the kid was hiding in there. He entered it, his eyes quickly scanning the room. Bunk bed with a superhero bedspread, toy chest, action figures, a soccer ball.

"Petey?"

But he knew instinctively Petey was not there. Still, he threw open the closet door. Toys and clothes overflowed the shelves and a red fire engine sat on the floor.

He closed the door, but as he started to leave the room, another picture of Petey and his dad caught his eye. Petey's father was tall with brown hair and had his arm slung around the boy, but in this photo he wasn't as clean-cut. His hair looked scraggly and long, and he sported a beard. Something about the look in the man's eyes and his appearance seemed familiar.

Like an undercover cop.

He should know. He'd let his hair grow long and used beards, mustaches, tattoos, anything necessary to fit in with the scum he was supposed to be part of.

Curious about Parker Stover, he hurried into Serena's office to look for more information on him, then dug through her file cabinet, but everything inside pertained to her business.

Had she thrown her husband's things away?

He had noticed a door in the hallway and wondered where it led. Maybe an attic.

A great hiding place for a little boy.

Spurned by adrenaline now, he flipped on the light and climbed the stairs. A few old pieces of furniture were stored in a corner, an antique chair, another bed, boxes of clothes and toys Petey had probably outgrown were crammed against another wall.

On the opposite side beneath the window sat an old trunk. Just big enough for Petey to crawl inside.

He crossed the room and opened it, hoping Petey was inside. Two worn blankets covered the top, then a lump.

"Petey?"

He felt beneath it, but his hand connected with a duffel bag instead of a child.

Frowning, he yanked it out with a curse and unzipped it. The damn bag was filled with cash.

All in hundred dollar packs.

His stomach knotted. Why in the hell did Stover have

this much money hidden in his attic? Did Serena know about it?

And where had the money come from?

He counted the first stack, and worry crawled up his spine as cop instincts filled in the blanks.

A large sum of cash like this suggested that Stover had been dirty.

UNABLE TO SLEEP, Serena's anger festered. She had been a cop's wife. She'd heard Parker talk about cases, had seen his methodical mind working to figure out the puzzles of a crime.

She had to help herself and do the same.

She called the deputy's name, and a moment later he surfaced. "You oughta get some sleep," he grunted.

Serena gripped the bars. "I can't. Would you mind giving me a pen and a piece of paper?"

His eyes narrowed. "What you gonna do? Try to break out with a pen?"

She rolled her eyes. "Don't be ridiculous. I couldn't overpower you if I tried." She forced a feminine smile. "But I would like to figure out who framed me. I thought I'd make a list of everyone who's been in my house the last few weeks and see if anything suspicious jumps out at me."

He studied her for a long moment. "I guess that'd be all right." He strode back to the front office and returned a minute later with a small yellow legal pad and a pen.

"Thanks."

He gave her a clipped nod, although she also felt his

gaze sliding over her as if he was judging her himself. A sense of how alone they were bolted through her, and perspiration broke out on her neck. The damn man might be handsome, but she would never use sex to obtain what she wanted.

She was well aware that some police officers and guards expected it. Even took it sometimes.

This bastard had been the one who'd handcuffed her and ripped her from her son and she would never forget that.

But he gave her a dismissive look, then walked away, and she breathed a sigh of relief. Maybe she was being paranoid. But her past had taught her that she had to remain alert, that she couldn't trust anyone.

As soon as he disappeared through the doors leading to the front, she sat down on the cot and thumped the pen on the pad, thinking. She didn't have any enemies that she knew of. But Lyle obviously had. Maybe he'd lied to her about what he did. Or maybe he had cheated someone in business and they wanted revenge against him.

She'd ask Colt and Kay to check into Lyle's past. Hopefully Colt was already exploring that angle.

Now, the evidence. Her panties and prints had been at Lyle's house. And the sheriff was having her van processed for evidence. What if they found something inside her van?

She frowned. Her prints could have been taken from anything, even a coffee cup or bottle of water. She and Lyle Rice had had coffee on their first date. She tried to remember—had she used a paper cup or glass mug?

Ceramic. She had also eaten a bagel, but she'd thrown the trash away when she was finished, and left the mug on the table.

Had they walked out together or had he lingered and slipped it into his pocket?

The memory slowly slipped into focus. He had received a phone call and stayed, and she'd left to pick up Petey from T-ball camp at the YMCA.

She quickly dismissed anyone from the Y. Most of them were young student volunteers or females. And the male coach had two boys of his own and no reason to frame her for murder.

So Lyle could have lifted her print from the mug, but if Lyle was dead, then someone else framed her. Had someone been watching him, planning his murder, then seen them together and decided she'd be the perfect patsy to take the fall? If so, he could have lifted her prints from the mug.

She closed her eyes picturing their movie date, trying to recall the details. She had ordered a Diet Coke and dropped the cup in the trash on the way out. But it seemed far-fetched that someone was following them to a movie and grabbed her cup. Still, if this killer was ruthless, it was possible. Something for Kay Krantz to point out in court.

The emails bothered her, too, but as Kay pointed out, someone else could have used her phone to send the emails. Or a professional might have the knowledge to set it up so it appeared the emails came from her phone when they actually hadn't.

But her underwear posed a bigger problem. Her

panties had to have been stolen from her house. She stewed over that problem. She hadn't noticed any signs of a break-in over the past few weeks.

So who had been in her house? Two of her clients had dropped off work, but neither of them had stayed or even come inside. She and Petey were so new to Sanctuary that he hadn't made a lot of playmates yet and she hadn't cultivated friendships either, so they hadn't had company. They'd been too busy settling in.

Only Lyle Rice had come inside to pick her up the night of the movie, and then to have an after-dinner drink.

Which meant that someone had broken into her house and stolen her underwear without her noticing. The thought sent another wave of fear through her.

When she was released, she had to change all her locks. She'd install a security system, as well. If she and Petey had been home when the person had broken in, he could have hurt her or her son.

She'd do anything to keep Petey safe.

COLT NEEDED to know more about Serena's husband and why he'd been killed. Could his death be related to Rice and his murder?

The bag of cash and both men having been murdered raised his suspicions.

He glanced at the clock. Five a.m.

Dammit, he had to find Petey. The poor little boy was out there somewhere alone, vulnerable. He scrubbed his hand over his bleary eyes. If anything bad happened to Petey, he'd never forgive himself.

Once again, he tried to climb in the boy's mind. He'd been sure Petey would run home. That would have been the most logical choice. Then again, Petey was scared and smart and probably realized that the police would search his house. So where else would he go?

Perhaps he had a friend he'd turn to. Or maybe Serena had a friend or sitter he liked...

He had to talk to her and confess that her son was missing.

He texted Derrick that he was on his way to see Serena, then locked up the house and headed to the jail. A minute later, Derrick replied that he'd meet him at the sheriff's office.

Only a few early-morning truckers hitting the roads for deliveries were on the road as he drove the short distance into Sanctuary. The sun was climbing in the sky, still half-hidden behind the mountains, and the air held a chill although the July heat would kick in by afternoon and the temperatures would soar.

He sucked in a sharp breath, berating himself again as he strode inside. Deputy Stone Alexander had nodded off in the chair, but he jerked awake, then rubbed his eyes. "What are you doing here so early?"

"I need to speak to Serena. Now."

Alexander dropped his boots to the floor. "You find her son?"

"No." Fresh guilt suffused Colt. "He didn't come home so I need to ask her if she knows where he might go."

Alexander nodded, then stood and grabbed the cell keys. They jangled in the silence as he escorted Colt through the double doors. The hall was dark, eerily quiet, and he wondered if Serena had finally fallen asleep. He hated to wake her, but she'd be furious enough that he hadn't come sooner.

Serena glanced up from the cot where she was scribbling on a pad when she saw him. She looked exhausted, as if she hadn't slept a wink, her eyes swollen and red from crying, mascara smeared.

Damn. Her nightmare was about to get worse.

"I've been making a list of questions." She rushed toward him. But his expression must have revealed that he had bad news because she suddenly went still.

"What is it? What's wrong?"

The deputy opened the cell door, and Colt stepped inside. "Serena, I hate to tell you this, but Petey ran away again."

"What? No." Anger and terror streaked her face and she stumbled backward and collapsed on the cot. "When? Where is he?"

"I don't know," Colt said. "Derrick said Petey finally settled down around midnight, then they went to bed. Derrick heard a noise around 2:00 a.m., and got up to check, but Petey was gone."

"No…" Serena shook her head in denial.

"Listen, Serena." Colt lowered himself onto the thin mattress beside her and gripped her arms. "I figured Petey might go home so I went to your house. I've been there all night hoping he'd show."

She took a shaky breath. "But he didn't?"

"No. Derrick has been combing the streets searching and so has the sheriff. Can you think of any place

Petey would go? Maybe a friend's house or a sitter's, somewhere he'd feel safe?"

Tears welled in Serena's eyes. "No…we haven't been in town long enough to make any real friends. And I haven't left him with a sitter yet." She gulped. "The only place he's been is at the Y for a camp."

Deputy Alexander cleared his throat. "I'll call the sheriff and have him check the Y."

Colt nodded his thanks, then footsteps sounded behind him. He heard Derrick speak to the deputy, then Derrick appeared at the cell.

"You…you were supposed to take care of him," Serena cried.

Regret and worry stretched across Derrick's face. "I know.… I'm sorry, Serena. Brianna and I are both torn up." He glanced at Colt. "Can I see you for a minute in private?"

Serena vaulted to her feet and pushed Colt's hands away. "Whatever you have to say you can say in front of me. I'm Petey's mother and I have a right to know what's going on."

Derrick's look turned tortured. "I…checked everywhere and couldn't find Petey, so I went back to the house and tried to figure out how he snuck out."

Colt's pulse clamored. "And?"

"The window was open. At first I thought he'd climbed through it, but I have a security system and couldn't understand why the alarm didn't sound. So, I looked around and discovered footprints outside the window."

"Petey's?" Serena whispered in a raw voice.

Derrick shook his head. "No, these were bigger. A man's."

Colt's blood ran cold as the inevitable clicked in. Someone had tampered with Derrick's security system. A man's footprints had been found outside the window.

Petey hadn't run away.

He'd been kidnapped.

Chapter Five

Serena trembled all over, her mind racing with panic. She had thought things couldn't get any worse.

But now Petey had been kidnapped.

Why was all this happening? Who would abduct Petey and what was the bastard going to do to him?

"Alert the sheriff, Derrick," Colt said. "We need a crime scene unit out at your place immediately, and he needs to update the Amber alert."

"I will. I just wanted to let you know first." Derrick glanced at Serena, his expression full of remorse. "I'm so sorry, Serena. Brianna and I only wanted to help. I don't know how this person broke in without us hearing...." His voice caught. "Brianna is worried sick."

Serena couldn't speak. She'd put her trust in these people when trust wasn't something she gave away, but now the situation was even worse than before.

Colt rubbed her arms. "I promise you we'll find him, Serena. I swear it."

Before he'd arrived, she'd finally pulled herself together enough to think rationally. Now all she could do was stare at him and imagine what might be happening to her son.

"I have to do something," Serena said, her voice warbling. "I should be out there searching. Maybe I could go on TV and make a plea…"

Colt glanced at the clock on the wall. "I'll call Kay and update her. It's only a few hours until you meet with the judge."

Serena's adrenaline kicked in and she clutched Colt's arms. "A few hours? In a few hours my son could be dead, Colt."

His dark eyes flashed with the realization that she could be right. "Under the circumstances, I'll see if Kay can move up the bail hearing."

She nodded, grasping on to that sliver of hope. "Get a picture of Petey from my purse and put it on the news. Maybe someone has seen him."

"I'll take care of it, call Kay Krantz and Gage and update the sheriff," Derrick offered, then rushed to see the sheriff.

"While the police get the search underway, we need to figure out what's going on," Colt said. "Lyle's alleged murder, your arrest, Petey's kidnapping—it all has to be connected."

Serena let that comment sink in. "You think someone killed Lyle, then framed me to get me out of the way so he could kidnap Petey?"

Colt shrugged. "That's possible although convoluted. You wouldn't have to be in jail for someone to kidnap him. Whoever took him could have just as easily kidnapped him from your place as Derrick's."

That was true. It had been riskier to break into a private detective's house.

Serena's stomach knotted. "Which means that the kidnapper really wanted Petey for some reason."

"Serena, can you think of anyone who would want to hurt you?"

Serena shook her head. "No."

"What about your juvenile record, the boy you assaulted?"

A shiver tore through Serena followed by a burst of anger. "I didn't assault that creep. He attacked me," Serena said. "His rich father paid the judge off and sent me to juvenile detention."

"Would he be evil enough to come back and try to hurt you now?"

She shook her head. "I haven't seen or heard from him in years. Last I did hear, he'd turned into a playboy and was living in California. I hardly think he'd take the time to come up with a plan like this."

"It does sound far-fetched," Colt admitted.

She showed him her notes. "I've been trying to determine how someone framed me. The fingerprints could have been lifted in public, either from my coffee mug where Lyle and I had coffee, or my soda cup at the movies. But my underwear had to have been stolen from my house. And other than Lyle, no one has been inside the house except for me and Petey since we moved in."

"How about repairmen? Salesmen?"

A memory tickled Serena's conscious. "Come to think of it, last week a cable truck was in the neighborhood, but the man didn't come inside." Her pulse jumped. "And another day some guy was cleaning gutters on roofs. But I didn't even open the door to him."

"Do you remember what either of these guys looked like? Were they in official trucks?"

"The cable guy worked for a local company with the logo on the side of his van. But the gutter cleaner was driving a beat-up white pickup truck. No logo or anything official on the sides."

"It might be nothing, but I'll ask Ben to check it out." He paused. "What else did Rice tell you about himself? Did he ever mention family? Where he was from?"

Serena twisted her hands together in thought. "He said his parents died years ago. After that, he moved around a lot."

"Did he receive any strange or suspicious phone calls when you were with him? Maybe a call that upset him?"

"Not exactly," she said, one incident springing to mind. "Although the day we had coffee, his phone rang as we were walking out. He seemed irritated and turned around and went back into the coffee shop to take it."

"You didn't hear who he was talking to?"

"No." She sighed. "I'm sorry, I'm not much help."

"You're doing fine." Colt offered her a tentative smile. "Serena, there's something else we need to discuss."

His voice sounded troubled. "What?"

"Your husband. You said he was shot in the line of duty. What exactly happened?"

Fresh pain gnawed at Serena. "He was DEA, working undercover. The police didn't explain exactly what happened, but essentially he was working on a drug deal that went bad."

"Drugs. Did he ever share any of the details about his work?"

She shook her head. "No, but the last few months he was troubled. Brooding. Moody. More secretive than before." Secretive to the point they had grown apart. She'd smelled perfume on him several times and wondered if he'd been having an affair. "I sensed there was something important he wasn't telling me, but when I asked, he just…shut down."

"Was his killer caught?"

Serena twisted her hands together. "Yes, he's in jail now."

A muscle ticked in Colt's jaw, and a frisson of alarm rippled up her spine. "Why are you asking me about Parker?"

Colt averted his eyes, and she sensed he was holding something back. "Colt, tell me."

He rubbed a hand over his chin. "When I was hunting for Petey at your house, I searched the attic and found a duffel bag full of cash."

Serena gaped at him. "Cash? How much cash?"

"At least a hundred thousand dollars, Serena. It raises questions about what your husband had gotten himself involved with."

"Maybe it was money for one of his undercover deals," Serena suggested.

Colt gave her a noncommittal look. "Maybe. But why would he have hidden it in your house?"

Serena's heart stuttered. She had no answer to that.

COLT HAD NO IDEA if the money or her husband's investigation was connected to Rice or her son's disappearance, but there were too many odd things that didn't add up.

Colt glanced at the clock again. "Serena, I hate to leave you alone, but I need to go to the office and talk to Ben and see what he's dug up on Rice. If his murderer kidnapped Petey, time is of the essence."

Serena straightened her shoulders and nodded. "Yes, of course, I'll be fine. Please go."

His heart ached at the torment in her eyes, and he cupped her face between his hands. "I promise I'll get to the bottom of this. And I'll be back for the bail hearing."

"Just find Petey," Serena whispered hoarsely. "He's all that matters."

"I will." Unable to resist, he drew her up against him for a moment, needing to soothe her as much as she obviously needed the comfort. "Hang in there, okay?"

She nodded against his chest, and he thought he felt tears dampen his shirt, but when he pulled back, her eyes were dry, her expression determined.

Deputy Alexander appeared again but kept his distance this time.

Serena tensed as she noticed him watching them. "Go, Colt."

Yes, he had to. Statistics proved every hour that passed lessened his chances of finding Petey alive.

The deputy cleared his throat. "Sheriff's updating the Amber alert," he said beneath his breath.

"Thanks." Colt paused. "Don't harass her, Alexander."

The deputy shot him a cold look, then Colt headed toward the front. The sound of the cell lock turning echoed in the silence behind him.

The sheriff met him at the door. "Everyone in the state should be looking for the boy now. The deputies in the county are organizing search parties. If he's in the town or mountains, we'll find him."

A small amount of relief worked its way inside Colt. "Thanks. We're going to need all the help we can get."

"The mother have any idea who would have kidnapped her son?"

Colt shook his head. "I have a gut feeling the abduction, Rice's alleged death, Serena's arrest—it's all connected."

Gray adjusted his belt. "We found fibers from an acrylic rug in Ms. Stover's minivan," Sheriff Gray said. "Forensics is working on comparing it to fibers from Rice's carpet. But my guess is the blood is a match."

"Doesn't this all seem too convenient?" Colt asked. "Like someone is trying too hard to tie Serena to a murder and make it look like an open-and-shut case?"

Sheriff Gray chewed the inside of his cheek. "Could be."

"There's no *could* about it," Colt snapped as he strode to the door. "You'd be a fool not to see it." He paused at the door and gave Gray a level look. "And I don't peg you as a fool, Gray."

"I'll do my job," Gray muttered. "You do yours."

The investigation would go faster if they worked together. Then again, if Colt found the bastard who'd framed Serena and kidnapped her child, he wasn't sure he wanted the law around.

Knowing he shouldn't waste a moment, he jumped in his Range Rover and sped toward GAI. Thankfully the buildings were close in proximity, and morning traffic was just kicking up. Not that Sanctuary had much traffic, but the few who were out had probably gathered at the diner for their homemade biscuits and gravy breakfast special.

He parked and rushed into the office and found Derrick and Gage waiting. "I still can't believe they nabbed the kid right out from under me," Derrick said, his voice riddled with guilt. "Bastard disarmed my security system. God, Brianna and Ryan were there, too."

"Don't beat yourself up, man. This guy is smart and determined," Colt said. "He orchestrated these details to frame Serena, so he must have been watching our every move."

"Let's meet in the conference room," Gage suggested.

When Colt entered, the other team members were there. Slade Blackburn, Amanda Peterson, Levi Stallings, and Brock Running Deer. The only one missing was Caleb Walker. He was on his honeymoon with his recent bride, Madelyn. Ben was in the corner working on his laptop, hopefully digging up something helpful on Rice.

"Gage filled us in," Amanda said. "How's the mother holding up?"

"She's tough but understandably upset," Colt said.

Slade steepled his hands. "Understandably."

Colt started with Serena's arrest and used a white-board to mark off the timeline of events from the moment Petey had asked him for help to Serena's dates with Rice and the confrontation the night of his alleged death. Next he listed the evidence the sheriff had compiled against her.

Slade thumped his boot on the floor. "Definitely smells like a setup."

"An elaborate plan to abduct a little boy," Amanda commented.

"There's something else," Colt said. "Serena's husband Parker Stover was an undercover cop with the DEA. He was killed two years ago when a bust went bad."

"Was his killer caught?" Gage asked.

Colt nodded. "Yes. He's in jail now for the crime."

Levi leaned forward, brow furrowed. "You think Stover's murder is related to Rice?"

"I don't know yet," Colt said. "But when I was searching for Petey at Serena's, I found a duffel bag of cash hidden in her attic. A hundred grand."

Slade whistled. The others' eyebrows raised.

"Did Serena know about it?" Derrick asked.

Colt jotted down the detail on the board and circled it. "No. She denies knowing it was there."

"It's a jump," Gage said. "But maybe Rice had a history of priors or a drug problem and knew Stover. And maybe Rice had a partner who knew about the cash and kidnapped the kid to get the money."

Amanda pursed her lips. "Then we should expect a ransom call."

Colt nodded. So far, they hadn't, though, which concerned him even more. "But if Rice's partner wanted the money and thought Serena had it, why not wait till she was gone and search the house instead of chancing jail for kidnapping?"

"Didn't you say that a pair of her underwear was stolen from her house?" Brock asked. "Maybe he did search the house and when he didn't find it, he concocted a plan to kidnap the child and ask for ransom."

"That's feasible." Colt still felt like they were missing pieces of the puzzle. "Then who killed Rice?"

Derrick cleared his throat. "The partner?"

Colt nodded, considering that theory. He turned to Ben. "Have you found anything?"

"Nothing on that van or truck in Serena's neighborhood," Ben said. "And at first not much on Rice. But I used some facial recognition software to change his appearance and look what popped up." Ben angled the computer to show Colt and the others his findings.

Several photos of Rice in varying disguises and with different hair colors and styles flashed onto the screen.

"Lyle Rice wasn't his real name," Colt said as he skimmed the information. "In fact everything Rice told Serena was a lie. He has several aliases."

"And a rap sheet," Ben pointed out. "He served time for fraud."

Colt's heart hammered in his chest. "Just look who the arresting officer was."

"Parker Stover," Ben said.

Colt whistled. "Looks like we just found our connection."

"WHAT IF THEY don't let me out on bail?" Serena asked.

Kay Krantz pulled Serena's hands into hers, then rubbed them with her own to warm her icy fingers. "Don't worry. He'll release you. Do you have access to cash for bail?"

She remembered the money Colt had mentioned finding in her attic and cringed. That money was probably dirty, and she didn't want any part of it.

But she had her husband's life insurance policy. Of course, she'd socked it away into savings for Petey's college fund and hated to touch it.

"Serena?"

"I could put up the house as collateral." She took a deep breath. "I'd like to save my cash in case I need to pay a ransom."

Kay nodded. "Right. I'll make that argument. We'll shoot for a low figure, but if we have to use the house, we'll do that.

"Colt called and explained about your son." Kay's voice caught. "I'm so sorry, Serena. But I know the detectives at GAI, and they're top-notch. They won't give up until they find him."

Serena nodded, her throat thick. She prayed he was alive when they did. She'd seen too many news stories to not imagine the worst.

Still, she had to remain positive. She had to do all

she could to find Petey. That meant being strong and helping Colt figure out who had abducted him.

Ten minutes later, they stood in the courtroom facing the judge. Serena felt like she was in a fog as the charges were read.

Kay requested bail be set at five thousand dollars, citing the fact that Serena worked in the community, had no passport, and that her son had been kidnapped.

"Sheriff?" the judge said, turning to Sheriff Gray.

"These are murder charges," Sheriff Gray said. "We have no reason to believe that Ms. Stover won't flee the state."

Kay cut him a stern look. "Give her a break, Sheriff. The woman's son is missing."

Colt tapped Kay's arm, then leaned over and whispered something. Kay nodded, then cleared her throat. "To satisfy the court and Sheriff Gray," she said, giving him a pointed look, "we'll agree that Ms. Stover be released into the custody of Colt Mason."

Serena tensed, but the judge set the bail, then slammed down the gavel, and Kay pulled her into a hug. "You're free, Serena. Now we just have to find the real killer so you can remain that way."

Before she realized what was happening, Colt had Serena's hand and tugged her toward the door. "Come on, Serena, we have to talk."

"Did you find Petey?"

"No, not yet." He shepherded her toward a parking lot adjacent to the courthouse, but suddenly the sound of gunshot rang out.

Serena screamed as Colt shoved her to the ground.

PETEY'S HEAD HURT, and his throat ached. He opened his eyes, but it was so dark he couldn't see anything, and a rag was tied around his eyes.

Where was he?

He tried to move, but his hands were tied together, and so were his feet. The terrible day and night flashed through his head. First his mommy being torn away and taken to jail.

Then the kid jail. And then Ms. Bri's house.

He'd been upset when they got there, and he'd wanted his mommy, but the bed had been so soft, and he'd been so tired and Mr. Colt had told him he should be nice to Ms. Bri. Then Ms. Bri gave him one of Ryan's teddy bears and he'd hugged it and fallen asleep.

But he'd woked up and that man had been in the room....

He sniffled. He wasn't at Ms. Bri's anymore.

This place smelled stinky, like rotten fruit or like someone had peed inside.

An engine rumbled, and he realized he was in some kind of car or truck. Maybe a van. He had to get out!

He belly-crawled across the floor searching for a door. But he smashed into a hard metal wall.

He crawled the other way, but hit another wall.

Then the engine fired up, and the van started moving. No...

How would his mommy know where to find him if the mean man took him away?

Chapter Six

Who the hell was shooting at them?

Colt covered Serena with his body, jerked his head up and scanned the parking lot and side of the building. Another bullet zipped by his shoulder, and he grabbed his Glock from inside his jacket.

"Serena, are you okay?"

"Yes. Who's shooting at us?"

"I can't see him, but he's in the alley." He gripped her hand. "Come on, keep low and stay behind me."

Shielding her again, he pulled her toward his SUV. Another bullet ripped past them and pinged his Range Rover. Suddenly guards from inside the courthouse raced outside, weapons drawn, searching the street.

He jerked his head, motioning toward the alley, but he heard footsteps, then spotted a man in dark clothing dart into a black sedan.

"Get in the SUV," Colt shouted. "And lock the doors." He threw her the keys, then chased after the shooter. A guard was on his tail, footsteps beating the asphalt behind him.

But the sedan sped down the alley toward the rear

exit. Colt fired, aiming for the tires, but the sedan was too fast and spun around the corner, disappearing from sight.

Colt paused at the corner, dragging in oxygen, and cursing beneath his breath.

The guard's breath rattled as he rushed up beside Colt. "Did you get a license?"

"No, no tag."

The guard flipped the radio mic on his lapel and called for assistance. "Shooting at the courthouse. Shooter driving a black sedan headed east out of town. Armed and dangerous."

"Did you get a description?" the guard asked Colt.

He wiped at the sweat rolling down his neck. "I didn't see his face, but he was big, stocky." He pivoted, searching the street again. "Check for bullet casings. I'm going back to Ms. Stover."

Leaving the guard to canvass the scene, he raced back down the alley to the parking lot. By the time he reached Serena, he was furious.

And even more certain that whoever had framed her and kidnapped her son had something to do with Rice's murder. And that it was connected to her husband and that money in the attic.

For the first time since the shot rang out, it occurred to him that there might have been a second gunman, and fear made his adrenaline kick in. He reached the SUV, and sighed in relief when he spotted Serena huddled low in the seat.

But when she looked up at him with those big, innocent, terrified eyes and he opened the door and found her trembling, he couldn't help himself. He pulled her in his arms again, and held her tight.

SERENA FELL AGAINST Colt, grateful at the moment to feel his protective arms around her. Colt slowly stroked her back, his own breathing choppy and broken.

"Did you catch him?" she whispered.

"No, but one of the guards called it in so the police are looking for his car now."

"Who was he?" Serena said against his chest.

"I don't know yet, and I didn't see his face. But all of these things have to be connected."

Serena inhaled his masculine scent and savored the potent feel of his muscular chest against her. She felt safe in her arms, and she hadn't felt safe with anyone in a long time.

Even those last few months with Parker, she'd known something had been wrong.

But the thought of getting close to anyone, especially a man, sent a frisson of fear through her. She couldn't get involved with Colt. He was a detective, only a fraction of a hair from being a cop himself.

And she'd sworn she'd never become entangled with another cop. Their job was too dangerous.

The very reason she'd thought Rice was safe. He was a businessman. Or so she'd thought.

What a horrible mistake.

The sheriff appeared from inside the courthouse, along with another guard. She saw Sheriff Gray jogging toward them, and forced herself to release her grip on Colt. But she immediately missed the comfort of Colt's arms.

Colt straightened as the sheriff approached, then buzzed the window down.

"What happened?" the sheriff asked.

"Someone fired at us when we came outside. I chased him into the alley, but he jumped in a black sedan and sped away."

"You two okay?"

Colt nodded, and Serena did the same, although anger was quickly replacing the fear that had seized her earlier. "What are you going to do about this, sheriff?" she asked. "So far, since you falsely arrested me for a crime I didn't commit, my child has been kidnapped, and now someone just tried to kill me. Do you still think I'm the bad guy?"

Sheriff Gray adjusted his sunglasses. "I don't know what's going on, Ms. Stover. But I intend to get to the truth."

Serena started to speak up again, but Colt squeezed her arm, and she wrangled her fury into control.

"I'm driving Serena home," Colt said. "Let me know if you track down the shooter, or come up with anything more on Rice's murder."

"Listen, Colt," Sheriff Gray said, his jaw tight. "I know you're investigating, as well, so keep me in the loop. If you interfere with the investigation, I'll bring you up on charges."

"I don't intend to interfere," Colt said harshly. "I intend to prove Ms. Stover is innocent and find her son and bring him back to her."

Serena's heart clenched, but the sound of Colt's determined and confident declaration helped to assuage her worries.

Still, Petey was missing, and they had no idea who'd abducted him or what the kidnapper's intentions were.

ON THE WAY to Serena's house, Colt phoned Ben and explained about the shooting. "Will you email me those files you did with the facial recognition software? I want Serena to look at them."

"Sure. Ben said the news story has been airing about Serena's arrest and Petey's kidnapping. We sent over photos of Rice, as well, and we've arranged for a tip hotline to come directly to us."

Colt sighed. "Thanks."

Ben hesitated. "The FBI will probably be showing up any minute."

"If they help Petey, they're welcome to jump in," Colt said. He turned onto Serena's street, and noted a media van parked outside. The beginning of the circus. "Dammit. The press is here."

Ben grunted. "Might not hurt if the public sees the terrified grieving mother."

Colt glanced at Serena. She had dark purple smudges beneath her eyes, her hair was tangled from their run-in with the shooter and she hadn't slept in over twenty-four hours. Plus, she was still wearing the jeans and shirt she'd had on when the sheriff had dragged her from her house in handcuffs the morning before.

She looked too exhausted and emotionally wrung out to deal with the press.

"Oh, God," Serena whispered. "They've probably plastered my face on the news and painted me as a murderer."

Colt gripped her hand. "When we get out, don't say anything, Serena. You shouldn't talk about your arrest or the case without your attorney present."

She squeezed his hand. "But I can ask everyone to look for my son, and I'm going to do that."

Pasting on a brave face, she opened the door, climbed out and walked up the sidewalk to her front door. A young woman with short wavy brown hair and a red pantsuit approached Serena with a mic, a pudgy cameraman behind her.

"Ms. Stover, my name is Lydia Feldman and this is Renny Delaney." She gestured toward the news van. "Is it true that you've been arrested for murdering a man named Lyle Rice?"

Colt rushed up beside Serena. "Ms. Stover is not at liberty to discuss the charges against her."

Lydia arched a brow at him. "Are you her attorney?"

"No, I'm a detective with GAI, and I'm looking for her missing son." He gave the woman a pointed look. "However, his kidnapping is a subject Ms. Stover would like to address."

A flicker of irritation at deflecting the first question morphed to interest at the mention of the kidnapping. This woman knew the public was hungry to see details on the child abduction.

Lydia adopted an appropriately sympathetic smile. "Ms. Stover, can you tell us about your son's abduction?"

Serena straightened her shoulders. "Someone broke

into the home where my son was spending the night and stole him from bed, that's what happened." Serena's face flushed with a mixture of emotions, and Colt stroked the small of her back, silently offering support.

"Have you received a ransom call or note?" Lydia asked.

Serena paled slightly. "No. Not yet. But I want whoever kidnapped my son to know that I will do anything, pay whatever you want, if you'll just bring Petey home safely." Her voice broke. "He's just a little boy. Please don't hurt him. Just give him back to me...."

The reporter's eyes softened then flew back and forth between Serena and Colt. "Do you have any idea who's behind the kidnapping?"

Colt stepped up and addressed the mic. "Not yet, but we suspect that whoever kidnapped Petey is the same person who framed Ms. Stover for murder. GAI is asking anyone with information regarding Lyle Rice to please come forward. My office has faxed photographs of him and Petey to the media. Although beware, Lyle Rice has used several aliases before and changed his appearance. Any background information on him or who might be behind his murder could prove helpful."

Serena reached for Lydia's arm and wiped at a tear. "And please, please, if you know anything about where my son is or who has him, call the police. I need him, and..." She paused to swallow back an onslaught of emotions. "He's only six years old. He needs his mother."

Colt gestured to Lydia that the interview was over. After all, Serena had said everything there was to say, and she'd said it perfectly.

SERENA FELT DRAINED as she entered her house. The sudden silence was a brutal reminder that her son was missing. There was no Petey running to greet her. No little feet stampeding across the floor. No laughter.

Only an empty hollow pit in her stomach and house and…her heart.

Her gaze swept the room. His cereal bowl still sat on the kitchen table, her coffee cup on the counter, taunting her with the fact that they'd been ruthlessly dragged from their home.

She suddenly felt dirty, violated, and needed to be alone. "I'm going to take a shower."

Colt sighed. "Sure. If you need to rest, Serena, lie down for a while. Then we need to talk again."

She wanted to ask him what more questions he could possibly have, but she knew there were more. Things she needed to think about. Her husband's past. That mysterious money.

Lyle Rice and his aliases.

But she didn't have the energy to do so yet, so she trudged down the hall. When she passed Petey's room and saw his toys, his unmade bed, the giant panda he liked to sleep with, her heart shattered.

Tears flowed like rainwater down her face, and she rushed to her room, tore off her clothes and threw them in the trash. She would never be able to wear those jeans and that shirt again without remembering the night she'd spent in jail wearing them.

A minute later, she stood beneath the hot water and soaped and scrubbed herself until she felt as if her skin was raw. The stench of the jail and those damn ink stains on her fingers haunted her.

Closing her eyes, she imagined that when she stepped out of the shower, Colt would be waiting in her bedroom smiling. That he'd tell her that her son was home safe and this nightmare had ended.

Finally when the water turned cold, she dried her body and tears and pulled on a pair of loose knit pants and a long-sleeved T-shirt, then blew her hair dry and yanked it back in a ponytail.

The scent of chicken soup wafted through the hallway, and she found Colt in the kitchen ladling the soup into two bowls. Apparently he'd raided her cupboard. He set crackers on the table, and she slumped down at the table, exhausted.

"Eat, Serena," Colt said quietly. "You have to keep up your strength."

Numb, she did as he said. Not because she was hungry, but she had to keep going. Had to stay strong. Had to help find her son.

She'd die without him.

Colt joined her, a tense silence stretching between them as they ate the simple meal.

"Thank you," she said when she'd managed to finish the bowl. Maybe she had been hungry. Who knew. Her emotions were on a roller coaster.

He nodded, then stood and took her bowl and his and rinsed them, then stacked them in the dishwasher. "If you need to sleep awhile, that's fine. I'll check in with GAI and see if they have any leads."

She propped her head on her hand, weary. "I can't

sleep. I need to do something, keep busy, try to figure out why all this is happening."

He nodded in understanding. "Then I want to show you that duffel bag of money and see if you recognize it."

Resigned, Serena stood and followed him to the attic. He crossed the space to the old trunk in the corner and opened it. Two blankets lay on top, and he pulled them back then removed a black bag.

She frowned, studying the outside of the bag, searching her memory banks to recall if she'd seen it before.

"Do you recognize it?" Colt asked.

She shook her head and watched silently as he opened the bag and the stacks of hundred dollar bills appeared. Shock settled over her. "I can't believe this was Parker's, that he hid it up here."

Anger bubbled inside her, and she paced to the attic window and stared out. Clouds were brewing in the sky, threatening a storm, making the sky look as dismal and gray as she felt inside.

A muscle ticked in Colt's jaw. "Had he brought cash home before like this?"

"No, at least not that I know of."

"If he was deep undercover," Colt said, "he could have planned to use it for a payoff, then bust the drug dealer. But he was killed before he could retrieve it."

That was the scenario she wanted to believe, but suspicions nagged at her, just as she was sure they were Colt. "I'm beginning to wonder what else I didn't know about my husband."

She stared at a squirrel skittering up a tree in the

yard, the tree where Parker and Petey had built his tree house, and her stomach churned.

"The last few weeks Parker acted differently. I was worried that being undercover had changed him. He seemed moody, distant, secretive, and I...thought..." She let the words trail off.

"Thought what, Serena?"

She sighed and ran a hand through her hair. "That he might be doing drugs himself."

Colt grimaced. "Sometimes an undercover cop is forced to do things he wouldn't normally do just to fit the role."

She shrugged. "His undercover job was driving a wedge between us. When he was here, which wasn't often, we argued a lot. I even...suspected him of having an affair."

"What made you suspect another woman?"

"Cryptic calls at all hours of the night. Hang up calls when I answered." She scrubbed at a smudge on the window. "Twice I smelled perfume on his clothes. And once I grabbed his cell phone when a call came in and saw a woman's name. Dasha."

"Did you confront him?"

"He said it was somebody he worked with."

"The woman could have been part of the undercover job," Colt said. "Let me show you something else."

"God, what now?"

He gave her a sympathetic look. "Let's go downstairs."

She fought the sense of trepidation overpowering her.

If Petey was missing because Parker had done something illegal, she would never forgive him.

Colt set his computer on the kitchen table, booted it up and opened a file. "Look at this photograph. This is the Lyle Rice you met?"

She nodded.

He clicked a few keys and various images of the man in different disguises appeared. "These are his aliases, at least the ones we've uncovered so far," Colt explained. "He had passports in several names, as well."

Serena watched the transformations, some subtle, some more extreme, in morbid fascination. "I can't believe this. He's a con artist."

Colt nodded. "He was arrested for fraud and spent five years in jail. Guess who the arresting officer was?"

The truth dawned on Serena, making her pulse pound. "Parker." She leaned closer to read the details of the arrest. "So Lyle Rice had a vendetta against Parker?"

Colt nodded. "It proves motive. And if he knew about that cash, maybe he cozied up to you in order to find it."

"Then someone murdered him," Serena concluded.

"You said the man who killed Parker is in prison. I'd like to pay him a visit and see what he can tell us. Maybe he has a connection to Rice. Could be Rice had a partner who killed him."

"So Rice's partner framed me to get me out of the way so he could look for the cash." She massaged her temple. "But why kidnap Petey?"

Colt shrugged. "Maybe he's going to ask for a ransom."

Serena worried her bottom lip with her teeth. "Then why hasn't he already called? And why try to kill me?"

Unless money wasn't the motive. He just wanted revenge against Parker.

Which didn't bode well for Petey.

Chapter Seven

Colt phoned Ben to discuss the connections between Parker Stover's murder and Rice. "Derrick is here. I'm putting you on speakerphone," Ben said.

"Colt, we didn't find any fingerprints outside my house or inside the room where Petey was sleeping." Derrick paused. "But I had plaster casts made from the shoe prints in the dirt. They were size twelve boots."

Now if they could only find those boots they might find the man. Or vice versa. "Thanks," Colt said. "I'm going to check out Rice's place, but I'll wait until dark." He didn't want the sheriff finding him unlawfully searching a crime scene. "And I want to talk to Stover's murderer. Can you give me his info?"

"Hang on a second." The sound of Ben clicking keys followed. "Stover's murderer confessed and is doing twenty to life in Central Prison," Ben said. "Name's Hogan Rouse."

"Thanks." Colt massaged a knot at the base of his neck. "Maybe he can lend some insight into Stover's undercover work and Rice."

"How's Serena holding up?" Derrick asked.

Colt sighed. "She's trying to be tough." Although he knew she was hurting. She was still staring out at the backyard as if she hoped Petey would magically appear from his fort or come riding up on his bike.

But the fact that there had been no ransom call had his nerves on edge.

"Bri and I feel terrible." Derrick's voice thickened. "Let us know if there's anything we can do to help."

"See what you can dig up on Rice's old cellmates. Maybe one of them can fill in some blanks."

"I'm on it," Derrick said.

Colt gripped his handset. "And put a trace on Serena's home and cell phone. If she gets a ransom call, maybe we can trace it."

Ben mumbled, "Got it."

Derrick made a low sound in his throat. "We have to find Petey, Colt. Bri and I know exactly how Serena feels. We're both blaming ourselves. For God's sake, I'm an agent and I let him get away."

"It wasn't your fault, Derrick." Colt swallowed hard. Petey had come to him, and he had let him down. "Let's stay positive and focus. We'll find him. We have to."

He only prayed it was in time, that the kidnapper hadn't hurt him already.

He would never forgive himself if he had.

Colt disconnected, and walked over to Serena. Her big sad eyes made his heart ache.

"Petey loves to play on that tire swing," Serena said. "And he and his dad spent hours building that fort. They even camped out in it the weekend they finished it. We grilled burgers and had a picnic and roasted marshmallows. Then we crawled in sleeping bags and watched the stars through the trees. I still remember Parker telling Petey about being in Boy Scouts when he was young." She sighed. "Petey said he wanted to grow up and be just like his dad."

"Your husband obviously loved Petey very much," Colt said, and found himself envying a dead man for the family who'd cherished him so much.

"So much that he put our lives in danger." Pain flickered in Serena's eyes as she turned to him. "What did Parker get us into, Colt? What could have been so important that he'd risk his life and ours for it?"

She paced across the room, flinging her hands. "Was he addicted to drugs? Did he suddenly become greedy and want the money? Or had he intended to leave me for this other woman?"

"Serena, stop." Colt crossed the room, gripped her arms and forced her to look at him. "Don't do that to yourself. We don't know what happened yet. Parker could have had good reason to have that money and for everything he was doing. When you work undercover, sometimes it's best, safer even, not to share your work with those you love. Keeping his two lives separate was probably his way of protecting you."

Hell, he didn't know why he was defending the man, except he had worked undercover and he knew firsthand how hard it was to walk that line. How hard it was to live two lives and not let one bleed into the other. How quickly dangerous criminals could come after a loved one in retaliation.

Serena dropped her head forward with a labored sigh,

and he pulled her up against him and wrapped his arms around her, soothing her. She leaned into him, and he rocked her gently. She smelled like fresh peaches and cream, and he itched to kiss her.

But that would be foolish. She was still grieving for her dead husband and terrified for her son.

"I'm heading to the jail to question the man who killed him," he said gruffly. "Derrick and Ben are also researching Rice's former cell mates. They might give us a lead."

Serena lifted her head and looked up at him. "I'll go with you."

She moved to grab her purse, but he gently closed his fingers around her wrist. Serena didn't belong in the same room with the filth housed in the maximum-security prison.

"No, you'll be safer here. Try to get some rest."

Serena shuddered. "I hope you can make him talk."

Gently he lifted one hand and stroked her cheek with his thumb. A flicker of something hot and needy flared in her eyes. His body reacted. His head screamed for him to walk away.

But the rest of him wasn't listening.

Instead, he tilted his head and gently closed his mouth over hers. One touch and his heart began to pound. She was tough in so many ways, yet sweet and tender in others, and he wanted to assuage her pain and feel her up against him.

She clutched his arms, her lips parting on a sigh

that sounded both weary and seductive, and his body hardened, aching to be closer to her.

SERENA'S BODY TINGLED with awareness and need as Colt teased her lips and thrust his tongue inside her mouth. He tasted bold and masculine, the pressure of his hard muscular chest against her breasts igniting a hunger that she hadn't felt in a long time.

A hunger that she hadn't expected to ever feel again.

The very idea sent fear running through her blood. But Colt moaned soft and low, and the sound caught in her throat, tasting so delicious that she couldn't drag herself away from him. The last two days had been a living nightmare, and for just a moment, she wanted to forget all the pain.

Colt cradled her face with one hand, angling her head to deepen the kiss, and she met his tongue thrusts with her own, savoring the seductive allure of the intimacy. His other hand skated down her back to her waist and lower to pull her sex into the V between his thighs. The bulge in his jeans was rock hard and potent, and resurrected an aching need to touch him more intimately.

But reality interceded with the trill of the phone. They jerked apart, her breathing ragged, her heart hammering. Remembering that her son was missing, guilt assaulted her, along with panic, and she ran to answer the phone.

"Hello."

Colt stepped up beside her, his black eyes still

glazed with hunger, but worry drew his mouth into a stern line.

"Serena, it's Joyce Hubbard, my God, I saw the news. I just can't believe what's going on with Petey. Have you heard anything?"

"Is it him?" Colt mouthed.

Disappointment ballooned in Serena's chest, and she shook her head to indicate it wasn't the ransom call. "No, Joyce. No word."

She covered the mouthpiece and whispered to Colt. "It's one of my clients."

"Tell her you need to keep the phone lines open," Colt whispered.

She nodded. "Joyce, I appreciate your call, but I have to keep the lines clear in case the kidnapper calls."

"Yes, yes, of course. Just let me know if there's anything I can do for you." Tears laced Joyce's voice. "Meanwhile, I'll start a prayer chain."

"Thank you, I appreciate that," Serena said. She could use all the prayers she could get.

Colt watched her with hooded eyes as she ended the call, and her lips tingled, craving his mouth again. She wanted comfort, wanted to lose herself to him, to feel his breath against her face and his hands on her body.

She needed to forget the hollow ache building inside her, an emptiness that intensified with every second that passed. She had lost Parker.

She could not lose her son.

Colt started to speak, but she shook her head. She didn't want to discuss what had happened between them.

She just wanted to repeat it.

And forget it at the same time.

Because she couldn't fill that hollowness with Colt Mason, a man of danger. No, she had to protect herself and her son from men like him.

She would use him to locate Petey. Then their relationship would have to end.

COLT SILENTLY CURSED himself for touching Serena as he headed outside to his SUV. He'd lost his senses for a minute when he'd kissed her. Had forgotten his job, that he was working for her.

That she needed comfort, not the man who was supposed to rescue her child pushing himself on her.

He could never replace her husband.

Not that he wanted marriage or a family, but she and Petey still loved Parker. And he could not forget that and become emotionally involved.

Except for a brief moment, he had forgotten she was part of a case. He'd been consumed by the idea of taking care of Serena and finding little Petey and helping them piece their lives back together again.

With him in that life.

Dammit. He pulled his hand down his chin. He was a fool.

He started the engine and drove through Sanctuary, then onto the highway leading out of town. Two hours to the prison—he needed that time to clear his head.

Just because Serena was the sexiest woman he'd ever met, just because he'd grown tired of the danger and living a secret life, and had almost lost himself in the process, didn't mean her husband had lost himself. That he'd turned dirty.

That *he* could have her and the family Parker Stover had left behind.

Hell, Stover might have been a damn saint. He had been a Boy Scout after all. Worked undercover. Put his life on the line for the greater good, to make the world a safer place. He built forts with his son and had cookouts and had given his life to the job.

Colt Mason was not about to walk in his shadow because he would pale in the light of day when the darkness inside him emerged.

Shutting off his emotions as he'd trained himself to do on the job, he focused on driving and the impending interview. Knowing most visits required an appointment, he phoned the warden at the prison and explained that he needed to question Rouse.

"I heard about the kidnapping," Warden Pierce said. "Believe me, Rouse is a cop killer. That don't exactly make him popular around here. But don't expect him to confess his heart out. He's not a talker."

"How about his cell mate? Or another prisoner he might have confided in?"

"Killed the last cellmate, so Rouse is just coming out of solitary confinement." The warden sighed. "Rouse doesn't have any buddies either. He's a loner through and through."

Colt grimaced. Interrogating Rouse might be a waste of time, but Colt had to pursue every possible lead. "Thanks, Warden, I'll be there in a couple of hours."

Colt stepped on the gas pedal and accelerated. Petey's life depended on him.

Just like his brother's had.

He'd failed his brother.

Petey was one kid he wouldn't let down.

DESPERATE TO BLOCK OUT the memory of Colt's kiss and purge her nervous energy, Serena scrubbed the kitchen. Tears blurred her eyes as she picked up Petey's cereal bowl. What if she and Petey never had breakfast together again?

She closed her eyes and mentally pictured her son sitting at the table dropping raisins onto his pancakes to make eyes and chocolate chips for a mouth, then opened her eyes and forced herself to believe that he was okay. That he would come home and they'd make those pancakes and go to the pumpkin patch in the fall and decorate holiday cookies for Christmas.

She dumped the milk and leftover cereal down the disposal, then rinsed and stacked the dishes in the dishwasher. Her coffee cup went next, then she scoured the sink, counters and table, willing the cleaning chemicals to wipe away the stench of the previous day.

On a mission now, she yanked the leftovers out of the refrigerator and tossed the remains, then washed the containers and wiped down the shelves.

But as she scrubbed, the memory of that money in the attic returned to plague her. Why had Parker left so much cash in the house?

And if he'd left cash, what else could he have hidden from her?

Spurred by questions and adrenaline, she dried her hands, then tossed the kitchen towel on the counter and hurried toward the attic. Late afternoon shadows slanted lines across the wooden floor and walls. Dust motes floated in the remaining rays of light, the scent of mothballs hanging in the air.

Tension knotted her stomach as she spotted the trunk again. Colt had buried the money beneath the blankets and locked the duffel bag inside the trunk. She paused, studying the items in the attic, trying to remember what she had kept of Parker's.

The first few months after his death, grief had nearly immobilized her. But after several months of seeing his clothes in the closet and knowing that he was never coming home, she'd forced herself to pack them up and donate them to charity. Parker's parents had both died in a car accident years ago, so she hadn't been able to pass on his certificates of merit and awards, but she'd boxed them up, thinking that one day Petey would want to have them as a reminder of his courageous father.

Torn over her feelings now, she half feared what she might discover.

But Petey's life was in jeopardy, and she had to face whatever Parker had been involved with to save her son.

Two boxes in the corner drew her eye. One held mementos of their first dates. She opened the first one and found dozens of photos of her and Parker at a ballgame, playing putt-putt, at a local fair and vacationing at the Outer Banks. Below the pictures, she scrounged through a cigar box filled with movie and concert ticket stubs, a menu from their honeymoon and a handwoven bracelet from Jamaica where he'd proposed.

Suspicions crept into her mind. He'd disappeared for hours that day in Jamaica. Had he been out making a drug deal?

Stop it, Serena. Parker was a good guy. Some criminal who wanted revenge on him is the one hurting you, not the father of your son.

She closed the cigar box, then dug through another box. Parker's favorite football jersey, an autographed baseball, Boy Scout badges, then his certificates from the police academy and a framed photograph of his captain giving Parker an award.

Nothing odd there.

Marginally relieved, she moved to box number three. This one held a few of Parker's books on criminal behavior, Parker's guitar and the army jacket Petey had insisted he would wear some day. She pressed the worn leather to her cheek, nostalgia overwhelming her at the familiar smell of leather and Parker's musky cologne.

Determined to stay focused, she folded it and set it aside, but a day calendar fell out of an inside pocket. Curious, she flipped it open and began skimming the dates and times, trying to understand the notations.

One initial kept popping out at her. D.M.

Meeting times and places scribbled in red.

D.M.?

The name of Parker's phone log flashed in her mind.

Dasha?

Anger railed inside her as she counted the numerous

times he'd met the woman. All late night rendezvous. All bars and motels.

Her heart throbbed painfully. She had been right.

Parker had been having an affair.

Maybe he'd planned to use the money in the bag to start his life over when he left her and Petey behind.

Chapter Eight

Colt showed his ID to the security guard at the gate and explained the reason for his visit. The guard radioed to the prison warden who cleared him to enter, and Colt rolled through the gates and parked in a visitor's spot.

The prison was a maximum-security facility housing the more dangerous criminals, with a wing dedicated to death row inmates. It resembled a castle, had been built by granite quarried outside the prison's east wall, and was situated on twenty-nine acres of land, enclosed by a double wire fence with razor ribbon on top.

Colt locked his weapon inside the dashboard of his SUV, then strode to the front of the visitor's center and entered. He stopped at the check-in desk and showed his ID, then was issued a numbered, laminated pass to wear into the main building. An elevator took him to the visitation center where a guard led him to a spacious room filled with numbered individual booths to offer privacy. Today wasn't one of the regular visiting days, so it appeared that he would have Rouse to himself.

Colt claimed the visitor's chair and watched as a guard opened the door and led a handcuffed and chained hefty guy with a shaved head and muscles twice the size of his own toward the opposite side of the Plexiglas. Rouse's leg chains rattled and clinked on the linoleum floor as he shuffled to his seat.

Scars crisscrossed the man's beefy arms and hands, his nose had been broken recently, and some kind of tribal tattoo snaked along the length of his right arm and up his throat to his chin.

Colt was a big man but this guy towered over him, and probably weighed three hundred pounds. The cold, lethal look in his brown eyes also indicated the man was just plain mean.

"My name is Colt Mason," Colt began. "I came to talk to you about Stover's murder."

Rouse simply glared at him as if Colt had interrupted something important he'd been doing. Maybe Rouse was planning which prisoner to kill off next. For a man on death row, what was one more murder on his hands?

"Two days ago, his wife was arrested for murdering a man named Lyle Rice." Colt watched for a reaction, but Rouse's body language signaled nothing.

"While she was in jail, her son, Stover's little boy, was kidnapped."

A brief twitch of Rouse's eyelid confirmed he'd snagged the man's attention. "I believe that Stover's alleged murder/disappearance and this kidnapping are all connected."

Rouse didn't move a muscle.

"You confessed to murdering Parker Stover?"

Rouse finally reacted with a slight shrug.

"I want to know the details. Why did you kill him?"

Rouse grunted. "Listen, mister, can't you read? It's all in the file."

"I know what's in the file," Colt said, jaw clenched. "You shot him in cold blood. What I want to know is the reason."

"File says that, too."

"It says you were paid, but not why the man who paid you wanted him killed."

"Didn't ask."

Colt knotted his hands. "Who paid you, Rouse?"

Rouse made a clicking sound with his teeth. "Don't know his name. Sent me ten grand in an envelope before the hit. Ten after."

"You never met the person who ordered the hit?"

Rouse grunted. "Don't work like that."

Colt crossed his arms and leaned back in his chair. "In light of this little boy's kidnapping, I thought you might grow a heart and remember something you forgot about at the trial."

Rouse cut his gaze sideways for a second, but when he looked back at Colt the dead, cold look had settled back into his eyes. "Nope. Can't remember what I never saw."

Colt's patience snapped. "So the person who hired you never indicated his motive for wanting Stover dead?"

"That's right." Rouse met his gaze. "Why should I care? Twenty grand is twenty grand."

"Did it have something to do with a drug deal?" Colt asked.

Rouse slammed his fists on the table. "I told you, I don't know."

The warden was right. Rouse was one cold bastard.

Colt chewed the inside of his cheek. "How about Rice? Did you know him? Could he have been the man who paid for the hit?"

Rouse's handcuffs clinked as he clenched his hands together. "Never heard his name."

Colt removed a printout of Rice's aliases and altered appearances, and held it up to the glass. "You may have known him by a different name. He's used several aliases. Did some time for fraud. Stover was his arresting officer."

Rouse growled. "Stover was a cop. Ain't no one in here too worked up over his death."

Colt racked his brain for something to offer Rouse in exchange for information, but what could he offer a man waiting to die? Especially a cold-hearted jerk like Rouse.

"So you're saying another inmate might have framed Stover's wife for murder and kidnapped her son as revenge? But why go to the trouble when the husband is dead?" He waited to see if Rouse would mention the money, but he didn't bite.

Instead he flattened his gaze.

Colt barely controlled his rage at the man's indifference. "Look, Rouse, if you know something about Stover or Rice or the person who framed Stover's widow and kidnapped the little boy, spit it out. You may not care about his father or helping his widow, but think about the kid."

For a fleeting second, Colt thought he detected a softening in Rouse's bleak eyes. Then the look disappeared and the anger returned.

Rouse pressed his face closer to the Plexiglas divider, then spoke in a low voice. "You're looking in the wrong place," Rouse said stonily. "Stover didn't get killed over no drugs."

Colt frowned. "Then what was he into?"

A vein throbbed in Rouse's forehead, accentuating a nasty scar. "Don't know, but heard some guys talking. Somethin' bigger's goin' down."

"What?" Colt asked.

Rouse stood, chains rattling. "Do your job and find out. I got stuff to do in here."

"Like what?" Colt asked, furious. "You're just waiting to die. Maybe you could save your soul if you helped this child."

"What are you, deaf?" Rouse shot him a condescending look. "I told you, find out what Stover was really doing and you'll find the kid."

SERENA STUDIED her husband's day calendar, circling the dates and times he'd met with D.M. Most of their rendezvous took place at night in bars, strip clubs and motels. Most in seedy locations.

Why would Parker have resorted to having an affair? Had she not satisfied him in some way? Was her love not enough?

Or had he just grown bored with her?

Stop jumping to conclusions.

Maybe D.M. was a man. But Dasha was not. Serena had heard her voice.

She could have been a drug dealer, though...

But why would the woman hang up when Serena had answered the phone if she wasn't Parker's lover?

The very idea that her husband had lied to her, that on all those nights while she'd waited on Parker, worried about him, trusted him, and loved him, he'd been screwing another woman, infuriated her.

Her phone jangled, and her pulse jumped. She raced to answer it, but checked the caller ID first. Another news station.

She'd already had three calls from newspapers across the States, and two from other clients. Disappointed, she let the message machine pick it up and paced to the mantel.

She studied the family photo of her, Parker and Petey, again wondering if the happy family she'd believed she'd had had been a figment of her imagination. When she'd lived on the streets, her experiences had taught her not to trust.

Yet she had trusted him. Had she been a complete fool?

Had Parker's undercover work taught him to lie so well that he'd tricked his wife?

DM. Dasha.

What if this Dasha woman had kidnapped Petey? Perhaps she'd wanted a family with Parker and decided to steal the son that had been left behind?

Worrying her bottom lip with her teeth, she paced

across the room again, contemplating that theory. But if Dasha had wanted what was left of Parker, why wait two years after his death to steal her son?

Her bones throbbed from fatigue and lack of sleep, but her mind refused to rest. Petey had been sheltered from the streets because she'd wanted to spare him the cruelty that others could inject upon those less fortunate or weaker.

Where was he now? Would he survive this ordeal? And if he did survive, would he be emotionally scarred for life?

COLT CHECKED IN with GAI as he neared Sanctuary. "Rouse suggested that Stover was investigating something other than drugs," Colt said. "I'm going to track down Stover's former partner and see if he can give us some information."

"Good idea," Gage said. "I'll call my buddy with the Bureau and find out if he has an idea what Stover had stumbled into."

"I looked into Rice's former cell mates," Ben interjected. "His first cell mate died in the pen. Second one was released on probation and has disappeared. A third one was killed two weeks ago in a boating accident off the coast of Florida."

Colt frowned. "Two dead and one in the wind? Sounds suspicious."

"Tell me about it," Ben mumbled. "Slade offered to interview the other prisoners who knew Rice. Maybe he'll come up with a lead."

"Thanks. I'm headed to Rice's house to search the premises. Maybe I'll find something the cops missed."

"It's possible," Gage commented. "Especially since they thought they had the killer in Serena and might not have dug too deeply."

"Any tips from the hotline worth checking out?" Colt asked.

"Not yet." Gage sighed. "We'll keep you posted."

Colt disconnected. Nearing Sanctuary, he took the turn toward the condo Rice had rented. Crime-scene tape glimmered beneath the moonlight as he approached, and he slowed, scanning the streets and perimeter for officers assigned to guard the scene, or curious spectators interested in a murder in Sanctuary.

Another possibility niggled at him. The murderer might return to the scene in search of evidence he'd left behind.

Or a lead to the money, if that had been part of his motive.

Colt parked down the street from the condo, tucked his gun inside his jacket for protection, then walked briskly between the rows of units, and circled to the back of the condo. A privacy fence encompassed a tiny yard. He scaled the wood railing, dropped to the bottom and crept toward the back entrance. Darkness shrouded the interior as well as exterior, but he removed a flashlight from inside his pocket and shined it on the lock, then picked it and slipped inside.

The temptation to turn on an overhead light or lamp to speed up his search was strong, but he couldn't chance a passerby spotting it and calling the cops.

He shined the flashlight across the kitchen. An L-shaped design with built-in appliances, but no evidence of food or recent use. A Formica table and two chairs occupied one corner, minimal furnishings that looked unused, as well. No family photos, personal touches or signs of Rice and his life in clear view.

The man had been in hiding. Probably methodically planning how to worm his way into Serena's life and exact revenge—and/or the money in the attic—from her. But his plan had backfired and he'd ended up dead.

A few bloodstains dotted the cheap linoleum, but Colt knew the worst was upstairs. Still, he needed information and began to dig through the kitchen drawers and cabinets, searching for a clue as to Rice's plans and who might have killed him.

Maybe an old girlfriend's number or something indicating a partner.

The kitchen drawers were stocked with cutlery, and the pantry held three cans of soup, a can of beans and some stale bread. The refrigerator was even more bare, the only item inside a piece of leftover pizza in a cardboard box.

He moved to the den, methodically scanning the room. A plain brown couch and chair, one end table and a small desk. He searched the drawer in the end table, but found it empty. The coffee table was stained with coffee cup rings, and a few magazines lay on top. The first three were finance magazines—had Rice used them as research to plan a new con?

The second magazine was a publication on coastal living featuring south Florida real estate.

Hmm, had Rice been planning a trip south?

He flipped through the pages searching for some indication of Rice's interest, maybe property that had been circled, but nothing stood out. Except hadn't Ben said that one of Rice's former cell mates had died off the coast of Florida recently?

He crossed the room and rummaged through the top desk drawer, but the only items inside were an assortment of take-out menus. The bottom drawer was empty. A blank notepad lay on top with a pencil beside it, but there were no notes or names or phone numbers listed. He checked the trash, but it had been emptied.

He wondered about Rice's car but assumed the police had impounded it. Maybe Gage could find out if they'd discovered anything inside. If he'd had a computer, they'd probably confiscated it.

Although Rice was a con artist, and Colt doubted he would have left a paper trail on his computer or evidence of his plans lying around.

Frustrated, he inched up the stairs. One bedroom, one bath. The double bed had obviously been stripped of the blood-soaked sheets and taken to the lab, but bloodstains still dotted the floor. He strode to the dresser and searched through the drawers. Socks, T-shirts, and three packs of unopened boxers were stacked neatly inside. The middle drawer and bottom drawers were empty. Moving to the closet, he noted three suits lined neatly in a row. He searched the pockets and linings in case Rice had sewn something inside, but again came up with nothing. Two pairs of dress shoes sat on the floor along with a pair of work boots.

Something about those boots niggled at his mind, and he checked the size. Twelve.

A frisson of unease hit him. The boot prints outside Derrick's house had been a male's, size twelve.

Size twelve was a common size, but still it seemed too coincidental not to examine further. He flipped them over and noticed leaves and dirt stuck in the grooves of the soles.

Was it possible that the kidnapper had worn these boots? If so, why bring them to Rice's apartment?

Other suspicions materialized as he analyzed the situation. Rice was a con artist. He'd tricked dozens of people out of their life savings, committed fraud, altered his appearances, created aliases and disguises and elaborate ruses to thwart the cops.

Could he have faked his own death, then framed Serena for his murder?

SERENA WAS ANTSY to hear from Colt. Maybe Parker's killer had given him a lead.

Or maybe he'd find something helpful at Rice's apartment.

The phone jangled and she clenched her jaw, praying it was the kidnapper, not another reporter. Or hopefully it was Colt with information. It trilled another time, and she raced over and glanced at the caller ID box.

Unknown.

She dropped her head into her hands and stifled a scream. It was probably a salesman.

Then again, it might be the man who'd stolen her son.

Nerves gathered in her stomach as she grabbed the handset. "Hello."

"Mommy!"

Serena's breath caught at the sound of her son's tiny voice. "Petey?"

"Mommy, help," Petey cried. "Please come and get me!"

She tightened her grip on the phone. "Where are you, honey? Are you all right?"

"Mommy…"

Footsteps pounded, then a loud bellow. "Give me that phone, kid."

"Petey, where are you, honey? Tell me, baby—"

Petey wailed, and she realized the man had wrenched the phone from him.

"Who is this?" Serena shouted. "What have you done to my son?"

The sound of Petey's cry reverberated over the line, and Serena's heart shattered.

"Please," she begged, "I'll pay you, give you whatever you want, just bring my son back."

But the phone went dead in her hands.

Serena sank onto the couch in despair. If the kidnapper wanted money, why hadn't he answered her?

Unless he'd never intended to ask for ransom money or bring Petey back at all…

Chapter Nine

Could Rice have faked his own death?

Once the idea wiggled its way into Colt's brain, it wouldn't leave. If Rice were alive, it would explain why the police hadn't found a body.

Other details ticked through his mind. Rice had been in Serena's house so he could have stolen her underwear, and the kitchen knife, and lifted prints from a cup or glass to plant at his house. He also could have planted those emails on her phone.

But why leave his shoes here to be found?

Because he'd assumed the police had already processed the scene and wouldn't return. His motive for the kidnapping was problematic, but the possibility of a ransom call still existed.

But the amount of blood on the floor and sheets perplexed him. Perhaps Rice had stored up blood to stage the scene. Or he could have stolen a few pints from a blood bank.

If so, the blood wouldn't have matched his own.

He needed to ask the sheriff to verify that the blood

type and DNA collected at the crime scene matched Rice's.

Energized by his theory, he searched the closet again, dropping to the floor to make sure he hadn't hidden something beneath the carpet, behind a loose board, or the top shelf.

Nothing.

One last room. The bathroom.

The bathroom cabinet contained the usual toiletries. Soap. Shaving cream. Toothpaste. Shampoo.

A used razor and a box of hair dye in the trash caught his eye. He examined the package—the color was sandy blonde.

In earlier photos, Rice's hair had been darker, almost black.

If Rice had faked his own death, he'd most likely alter his appearance so no one would recognize him. Colt dropped to his knees and dug through the trash again, but barring a Q-tip and a tissue, he found nothing. Just as he was about to stand, he spotted a loose tile behind the back of the toilet.

He removed his pocketknife from his pocket, flipped it open and pried the tile loose. A second one came free, revealing a small hole carved in the wall. Colt dug around until his fingers closed around a small pad.

His heart jackhammered. No, not just a pad, but a ledger. Maybe the details inside would lead to Rice and his plans.

Columns of dates and what resembled GPS coordinates lined the pages. Another column was filled with numbers and letters, but he couldn't discern their significance.

The notations were obviously entered in some kind of code.

Anxious to get the ledger to Ben to decipher, he jammed the ledger inside his jacket, then replaced the tiles. Shutting off his flashlight, he made his way to the kitchen again.

The headlights of a car fanned across the front, and he ducked down and inched into the kitchen. He paused at the door and glanced back at the front window to make certain the cops hadn't arrived, but the car slowed, then moved on.

Relieved, Colt let himself out the back door, then eased open the fence, and dashed behind the bushes just as another car drove by.

He'd switched his cell phone to silent, but it was vibrating, and he checked the number. Serena.

He closed his hand over the mobile unit and darted behind the other condos, then to his SUV. Just as he shut the door, his phone vibrated again, and he connected the call. "Serena?"

"Colt, Petey called," Serena said in a choked voice. "He's alive, but the kidnapper grabbed the phone before he could tell me where he is."

Sweat beaded on Colt's neck. "Did he ask for a ransom?"

"No," Serena cried. "He hung up."

Colt clenched the steering wheel with a white-knuckled grip. That was a bad sign. Various scenarios surfaced, different cases he'd heard about on the force.

The horrific things child predators did to children. The mental and physical abuse. Murder.

This kidnapper wasn't motivated by money or he would have stayed on the line.

Which meant that he either intended to kill the boy or pass him on to someone else.

Roy Pedderson had kidnapped Sara Andrews to give to his sister. But Colt had a bad feeling this perp hadn't abducted Petey for a relative.

The other possibilities made his skin crawl.

SERENA STARED at her cell phone and the landline, willing them to ring. Willing the kidnapper to call back and ask for money, to promise that he'd return her son to her alive.

Poor Petey… He'd sounded terrified.

Would the kidnapper punish him for calling home?

Various scenes from TV shows of abducted and exploited children taunted her along with her own painful memories of the streets, and she broke out in a cold sweat.

She'd been older when she'd run away from the last abusive foster home, but she'd still ended up in trouble. She hated to think what her little boy might be enduring now.

A car engine puttered, and she checked the window. Colt whipped his Range Rover into the drive and jogged to the front door. Grateful not to be alone anymore, she threw open the door.

Storm clouds gathered on the horizon, a stiff wind scattering leaves and bending tree limbs. The breeze also caught the strands of Colt's black hair and made them stand on end. He kicked dirt from his boots onto the doormat and stepped inside.

"Did he call back?" Colt asked.

Serena shook her head. "No. I'm afraid of what that means, Colt."

He cut his eyes away, and she realized that he shared her fears. Then the steel was back in his expression, his angular jaw taut.

"Focus on the positive. We know he's alive." He removed a small leather ledger from inside his jacket. "I might have a lead on the con Rice was working on. I need to take this to Ben at the office ASAP."

"What is it?" Serena asked.

"A ledger with dates and GPS coordinates in it, and some other information, but it's in a code. Hogan Rouse, the hit man who shot your husband, said that Parker wasn't killed over drugs, that something bigger was going down. That if we figured that out, we'd find Petey."

Serena's pulse clamored. "Did he tell you what Parker was investigating?"

Colt shook his head. "Said he didn't know. But this ledger might be the key."

"Then take it to GAI now." Serena remembered the date book she'd found in Parker's things and hurried to retrieve it. "Look at this, Colt. It was in Parker's things. There are dates and places of meetings he set up. The initials D.M. are in here repeatedly."

"Do you know who D.M. is?"

"No. But I told you about that phone call from the

woman, Dasha. If you look closely at the meeting places, they're bars and hotels. My guess is D.M., Dasha, was Parker's lover and these were their rendezvous times and places."

"Maybe, maybe not," Colt said. "But she might have information about Parker's investigation. What about his partner? He might know about both."

Serena frowned. "Geoff Harbison?"

Colt nodded. "Detectives share things with partners they can't share with families. Maybe he can help us."

Serena nodded. Although she hadn't seen Geoff since Parker's funeral. "It's worth a try." She shoved the date book in his hands. "Show it to him. I have to know the truth."

"I want you to go with me," Colt said. "When we leave GAI, we'll confront Harbison. He might feel more compelled to open up if you were present."

Geoff's face flashed into her mind. He'd paid his respects at the funeral, then literally walked out of her life. Not that she'd expected the older guy to visit her and Petey, but she had expected *something.* He'd worked with Parker for five years outside of Raleigh and had a wife and son of his own.

Then she remembered the call from Petey, and panic set in. "But what if Petey or the kidnapper calls back? I have to be by the phone."

Colt rubbed her arms with his hands, his look determined but reassuring. "I set up a trace on your cell and landline, and arranged for your home phone to automatically be forwarded to your cell if you're not home."

Serena inhaled a calming breath. "Then let's go."

She had survived foster care and the streets. She would survive now and beat down those same streets herself if that's what it took to find her son.

FIFTEEN MINUTES LATER, Colt and Serena met with the agents at GAI. "I found this ledger at Rice's apartment. I'm hoping you can decipher it."

Ben narrowed his eyes as he studied the columns of information. "It might take a little while, but I'll see what I can do."

"Thanks." Colt shifted and turned to Slade. "Did you learn anything from Rice's cell mates?"

Slade shrugged. "Just that he went from one con to the next, and was always looking for the next score. Each one had to be bigger than the last." He drummed his fingers on the desk. "Only woman they mentioned was some girl who wrote him in prison a couple of times. Her name was Candy."

"Last name?" Colt asked.

Slade made a sarcastic face. "Kane."

Colt rolled his eyes. "Did you find her?"

"Dead end. The address she wrote him from was California. Tracked down her old roommate and she said Candy is a stripper and cokehead. She overdosed six months ago."

Damn. Colt hadn't shared his theory about the possibility of Rice being alive with Serena, but he had to now. "There's something else. Gage, can you make sure forensics analyzed the blood on the sheets at Rice's apartment and find out the results?"

Gage leaned back in his chair and folded his hands

behind his head. "You have some reason to believe it's not Rice's?"

Colt hesitated. "Maybe. A few things about this case just don't add up. First, there was no body. And second, we know Serena didn't murder Rice, drag his body from his room and dump him. So who did?"

"Good question," Derrick muttered.

Colt shifted. "When I was at Rice's I noticed a razor and hair dye box in the trash."

Derrick shrugged. "Rice was a master of disguise. He could have altered his appearance to escape, but he was killed before he had a chance to get away."

Colt chewed over that theory. "True, but why didn't the CSI unit take the hair dye package and razor for processing?"

Amanda cleared her throat. "Are you suggesting that Rice isn't dead? That he faked his murder, then came back and changed his appearance after the police were at his apartment?"

Serena gaped at him, obviously stunned. "Why would he go to all that trouble to frame me?"

Colt clenched his jaw. "Like we said before. Maybe he wanted revenge against your husband. Having you arrested cleared the way for him to kidnap Petey."

"So if Rice faked his death," Amanda cut in, breaking the awkward silence, "then where did all that blood on his sheets and floor come from?"

"Exactly the reason I want the blood tested," Colt continued. "For all we know, Rice could have saved his blood to plant it there. Or the blood could be an animal's." He paused. "Or if Rice had a partner, he could have killed his partner, gotten rid of the body, then made it appear as if he'd been murdered instead."

"So no one would look for him," Derrick said in disgust.

"Makes sense. It would explain why Rice's body hasn't been recovered," Slade said, picking up the thread.

"And how evidence against Serena showed up," Gage added. "Rice stole evidence from your place, Serena, then planted it at his house."

Colt showed them the evidence bag holding the pair of boots. "These boots were in Rice's closet. Size twelve. They have dirt and grass caked in the soles."

Derrick stood. "Let me have them analyzed and see if they match the prints taken outside my house. I'll also see if there's DNA inside to verify that Rice wore them."

"But why would Rice kidnap Petey if not for the money?" Serena asked.

A tense heartbeat passed while everyone considered that question.

No one, including Colt, liked the answer.

SERENA LAPSED INTO SILENCE as they drove toward Geoff Harbison's house near Raleigh. Petey's terrified voice echoed in her head, tormenting her.

Would she ever see him again?

She clenched her hands in her lap. How could she have been so foolish to get involved with a devious man like Rice?

If Rice had faked his own death, he had methodically

planned every detail. The first time they'd met, the coffee, the invitation into her house to steal her things. Maybe he'd even copied her key so he could come and go at will.

She struggled to remember the sound of the kidnapper's voice, the intonation, but she'd been so focused on her son that she couldn't recall the details. Could that voice have been Rice's?

Had he abducted her son, then returned to shoot at her and Colt outside the courthouse?

Her lungs tightened. If he wanted her dead, that meant he had no intention of returning Petey....

Dear God, what was he going to do with her son?

Chapter Ten

Colt slipped his hand over Serena's, and she ached to hold on to him. But how could she trust any man when it appeared her husband might have deceived her as well as Rice?

"We're going to find Petey," Colt said gruffly. "You have to keep telling yourself that. You can't lose faith."

"I don't know what I believe anymore," she said on a pained sigh. "It seems like everyone I've ever known has lied to me."

"I promise never to lie to you," he said in a husky voice.

Serena sensed he meant it, but what if he already had lied? What if they didn't find her son?

Their earlier kiss teased her mind, and she pulled her hand free from his. That kiss had felt too good, too tempting. Too selfish.

She couldn't rely on Colt or anyone else, or put her own needs before Petey's.

Hadn't the streets taught her about survival? Sure, she'd softened after she'd married Parker. She'd allowed him to take care of her and Petey, but then he had been murdered, and they were alone, on their own.

If she'd stayed on her own instead of allowing Lyle Rice into her life, she and Petey would be safe at home now.

Colt steered the vehicle into a small neighborhood of older homes. Although night had set in, the moon glimmered, revealing a mixture of small brick ranches mingled with clapboard houses, some with peeling paint and sagging awnings. Even so, most of the yards were well tended and signs of children sprang up in the toys and outdoor play equipment in the yards.

Serena twisted her hands in her lap. "Geoff knows we're coming?"

Colt nodded. "I phoned on my way to your house. Do you two keep in touch?"

"No." Serena noted the handicap ramp on the side entrance and remembered that Geoff's son had cerebral palsy. "The last time I saw Geoff was at Parker's funeral. I guess he's been too busy to check on me and Petey." Besides, he had his own family and problems and hadn't needed hers dumped on his shoulders.

She almost hated to bother him now.

Colt parked, and Serena noticed the withered flower beds and parched grass as they made their way up to the front door. Colt rang the doorbell, and a ding sounded, then the sound of a dog barking followed. A second later, a golden retriever bounded up to the glass window closest to the door and pressed his nose against the glass.

Footsteps followed, and the door swung open. Geoff stood in the doorway wearing an ill-fitting T-shirt and baggy pants, his face craggy and weathered.

The dog barked, and Geoff patted her back. "Go to Billy, girl, go on." The dog turned and trotted away.

Serena frowned. Geoff looked as if he'd aged ten years since she'd seen him at the funeral. Dark pockets were carved beneath his gray eyes, his hair had grayed and looked shaggy, and he'd lost weight.

He glanced at Colt, then a weary sadness flickered in his eyes at the sight of Serena. "Hello, Serena."

"Geoff, it's been a long time."

He nodded and cast his face downward as if ashamed. "I know, I'm sorry." His voice caught, then he cleared his throat. "I heard about Petey. That's awful."

Serena nodded, biting her lip to stem tears.

Geoff, shifted, obviously uncomfortable, then angled his head toward Colt. "You must be Mason, the detective who called me."

Colt extended his hand and Geoff accepted it. "Yes, sir. Colt Mason, GAI. Thank you for seeing us."

Geoff rubbed an age-spotted hand across his chin. "Come on in. I'll get us some coffee."

The whir of a wheelchair echoed, and Serena spotted a dark-haired boy with a big smile, probably about ten although he looked small for his age, hunched in the wheelchair. "Pop, the ninja is about to attack."

Geoff forced a tight smile. "Okay, son. But Pop has company now." Geoff gestured toward the room to the right. "Go back in the den and finish the movie. I'm going to chat with these people for a few minutes."

The boy's face fell slightly. "I can pause the movie till you're finished."

Geoff glanced at his watch. "If you do, you won't have time to see the end before bedtime."

Serena almost laughed at the torn expression on the child's face. "Okay, but I'll watch it again with you this weekend."

Geoff nodded. "Deal." The boy spun the wheelchair back around, and zoomed into the den, and Serena and Colt followed Geoff to the adjoining kitchen. Geoff handed them coffee in chipped mugs, and Serena toyed with the handle as he lumbered into a seat across from them.

"I don't know how I can help you," Geoff said as he dumped sugar in his coffee. "I retired a year and a half ago and spend my days taking care of Billy now."

"Where's your wife?" Serena asked gently.

Geoff's mouth drew into a frown. "Lost her to a heart attack two years ago. It's been rough since. Billy needs constant care, physical therapy. I couldn't keep on the job and take care of him, too."

Serena covered his hand with hers. "I'm sorry, Geoff. That must be hard."

His gaze met hers and moisture filled his eyes. A moment later, he pressed his lips together and straightened, blinking away the tears. "You have any idea who took your little boy?" Geoff asked.

Serena shook her head.

Colt explained the chain of events and his most recent suspicions. "Rouse suggested that Parker Stover was investigating something bigger than drugs, and that investigation got him killed. You and he were partners. Did he confide in you what he was working on?"

Geoff stared into his coffee for so long that Serena thought he wasn't going to answer. Finally he cleared his throat. "Yeah, we were partners, but my life was complicated back then...and Parker. He didn't like to talk about his undercover work."

"Geoff, please think," Serena pleaded. "We think Lyle Rice was connected to Parker's death, and that Rice or his partner framed me and kidnapped Petey."

"I don't know anything about Rice," Geoff said. "Parker was working a narcotics ring, but said he stumbled on something else that he suspected might be big. But he never confided the details. In fact, he became real secretive toward the end. I pushed him to tell me what was wrong, but he wouldn't talk to me." He took a sip of his coffee. "Then again, he was undercover and Parker was good at playing a role."

"Just like Rice," Colt muttered.

Serena felt a stab of pain in her chest. She wanted to defend Parker, but he had been a skilled liar. He'd had to be or he never could have worked undercover.

Colt cleared his throat. "Did he mention any suspects' names?"

Geoff shook his head. "Just said that he was using the cash from one of his busts to front another deal. One for a shipment of some cargo that he wanted to stop."

"Cargo?" Colt asked. "What could be bigger than drugs?"

"Diamonds was my guess," Geoff said. "Maybe from Africa."

Blood diamonds, Serena thought. "Then why didn't he bring you into the investigation?"

Geoff shrugged. "He said he needed more before he could make an arrest. He didn't just want the little guy. He wanted the master behind the plan, and he was close to getting him."

"But he was killed before he made the arrest," Colt said.

Geoff nodded and pushed his coffee away, his expression tormented. Serena wondered if he blamed himself for Parker's death. Maybe that was the reason he hadn't kept in touch.

She drew Parker's date book from her purse. "Geoff, I found this in Parker's things. The initials D.M. keep popping up. This woman named Dasha phoned a few times, as well. She always hung up when I answered." She paused, her heart thumping off beat. Did she really want to know if Dasha was her husband's lover?

Yes, she had to know the truth. It might lead her to her son.

"Was Dasha the D.M. Parker kept meeting at these bars and hotels?"

Geoff glanced at the date book, anxiety tightening his craggy features. "Yes."

Serena sucked in a sharp, pain-filled breath. "Were she and Parker having an affair?"

Geoff jerked his head up. Then slowly he shook his head. "No, Serena, it wasn't like that. Dasha wasn't Parker's lover. She was his confidential informant."

COLT SAW THE RELIEF on Serena's face, and realized she still loved her husband.

Another reminder that he could not fill the man's

shoes. Nor did he want to try. When Serena had Petey back, she wouldn't need him anymore.

And he'd suffered enough loss in his life. He wouldn't fall for a woman who couldn't return his feelings.

"Do you know Dasha's last name or how we can find her?" Colt asked.

Geoff shook his head. "You might check some of those places in his date book. They always met up in a bar or hotel late at night outside of Raleigh. Part of her cover and his."

"You mean she dresses like a street girl?" Serena asked.

Geoff's eyebrows rose. "If that's what you call a prostitute, yeah."

"Thanks," Colt said. "You've been a big help."

Geoff stood and tugged at his pants, then glanced at his son with an odd look on his face. "I wish I could have done more. Saved Parker."

Serena circled the table and gave him a hug. "Don't blame yourself, Geoff. Parker died doing his job. He knew you had his back."

Colt thought he saw a frisson of guilt enter Geoff's eyes, but being partners was like being brothers, and he understood that kind of guilt.

Serena released him and walked toward the door. "Come on, Colt. Let's see if Dasha knows what my husband was up to and why he was killed."

Colt didn't want to take Serena to those seedy places. "Listen, Serena, let me drive you home. I'll hit those bars and hotels alone."

Serena threw him a look of dogged determination as

she strode out the door. When he caught up with her, she stopped on the porch stoop and planted her hands on her hips. "Colt, I realize you want to protect me, but you're wrong about me. I grew up on the streets. Believe me, I know how to survive there." A haunted look darkened her eyes. "Besides, it will take too long for you to drive back to Sanctuary and then here."

She hurried to his Range Rover then, leaving him to wonder what she meant. Her comments about her juvenile record and growing up in foster care echoed in his head.

Serena was complicated, loving but tough—a lethal seduction.

His phone buzzed, and he yanked it from his belt and checked the number. Gage.

He quickly punched the connect button. "Yeah?"

"Colt, Caleb Walker just called. He may have some information."

"Caleb? I thought he was on his honeymoon."

"He just arrived home. Anyway, his wife's twins have some kind of psychic gifts that connect them."

"Yeah, I remember. But what does that have to do with this case?"

"Cissy, one of the little girls who was missing, saw the news report about Petey and Lyle Rice." Gage sighed. "She said she recognized Rice, that she saw him talking with Ray Pedderson."

"Wait a minute. Pedderson was the one who kidnapped her, right?"

"Right. She also claimed that Pedderson put her in

a truck to haul her around, that in the truck she sensed other kids had been tied there before."

"You mean Rice might have been connected to the illegal adoption ring Dr. Emery started?"

"I don't know." Gage muttered a sound of frustration. "It may mean nothing, but that's one more question I'll ask Mansfield, the sleaze-bag lawyer. We still think he knows more about Emery's operation than he let on."

Colt rubbed his chin. "Keep me posted."

He hung up, his own mind racing with questions. Pedderson and Rice and Mansfield might have been working together.

Another piece of the puzzle to figure out. Had they gone from small abductions for local adoptions to an international kidnapping ring?

SERENA CHECKED her phone for the hundredth time as Colt drove them toward the bars.

It would be the second night Petey had spent away from her. The second night since he'd been torn from her arms.

Her chest tightened. Her little boy could be miles and miles away by now, in another state even. And if Rice was alive and had a passport and new alias, he might even take him out of the country.

No…she couldn't let her mind go there.

Hopefully Dasha knew something that could lead them to her son.

Research Triangle Park was a mecca for technology, business and college life and between Raleigh,

Durham and Chapel Hill, boasted shopping centers, fine restaurants and dozens of bars.

"So where is the red-light district here?" Serena asked.

Colt gestured toward his left and turned down an alley. Serena spotted several empty warehouses that had fallen into disrepair and a couple of seedy bars.

"You've been here before?" Serena asked Colt.

He gave a clipped nod. "When I worked undercover, I ran down some gun deals here."

Serena nodded, his comment a reminder that his job was too much like Parker's.

She forced her mind on to the task. It was early evening, but already a fake-boobed, dyed blonde with thigh high boots, fishnet stockings, and a tank top that dipped down to her navel stood on the corner scoping for johns.

Colt slid into a dusty parking lot, and Serena glanced up at the neon signs for the bar, old memories of her life before taunting her. She hadn't always been proud of what she'd done. She'd stolen money for food when she'd been desperate, had scrounged for day-old bread from bakeries who prided themselves on daily fresh baked goods, and had slept in abandoned houses and buildings just to survive. But she'd never sold herself for sex, and she felt sorry for the girls who resorted to that low.

But Colt didn't need to know any of that, so she adopted her game face. Tonight was not about her. It was about finding Petey and bringing him home safe.

She reached for the door handle. "I'm thirsty. How about you?"

He quirked a brow. "Sure. Let's go."

She opened her door, ignoring the rancid odor of garbage and urine as they wove along the alley. The moon fought to push its way through the dark clouds but lost, casting the night with the gray bleakness of despair and doom.

She passed a homeless man curled on top of a piece of cardboard, dug in her purse and dropped five dollars into his hand. "For food," she said, knowing he might use it for booze. But it was his choice. Whatever fed his weary soul.

He reached up and patted her hand, his eyes full of emotion and the haze of too long having been shunned. "God bless you, girl."

"You, too." Serena smiled at him, remembering the kind old lady who'd taken her in after the juvenile center. Miss Birdie. She'd told Serena her own sad story about the street life, then claimed that one day she'd found Jesus and it had changed her life. She'd kicked the booze habit and decided to help others instead of wallowing in her own grief.

Serena had cried her heart out the day the poor woman had died. But she had been grateful for those years for they had inspired her to turn her own life around. Miss Birdie had made her believe in family and that she deserved to be loved, to have a family of her own.

She glanced down at her clothes. Her jeans and conservative shirt were great for mothering but not for attracting attention at a bar. She removed her ponytail holder and fluffed her long hair, giving it a tousled look, then knotted her T-shirt below her breasts, exposing her stomach. A quick swipe of lipstick added to the party girl look.

Colt arched a thick brow, but didn't comment as the blonde approached him and stroked his arm seductively. "Hey, handsome, what can I do for you?"

Colt offered her a smile. "We're looking for Dasha. You know her?"

The blonde pinched her collagen-enhanced lips together. "Damn that girl, she gets all the cute ones. I ain't seen her tonight." She stroked his jaw with her bloodred fingernail. "You sure I can't help you, honey? I ain't had no complaints yet."

"Thanks, sugar, but I really need Dasha." Colt folded a twenty-dollar bill into her cleavage. "When she shows, tell her to find me inside."

Serena maneuvered past them and inside the bar. Cheap beer and booze flowed, laughter, jokes and loud music blaring. Two tattooed men with beer guts by the jukebox whistled at her while a younger skinhead looked up from the pool table and gave her a once-over. Obviously deciding she wasn't worth his time, he returned to the game.

Serena claimed a barstool and ordered a draft beer. Colt did the same, his gaze scanning the room. A biker in a leather vest and jeans with shoulder-length hair straddled the stool on the opposite side of her.

"Can I buy you a drink?"

Serena opened her mouth to speak but Colt cut in. "She's with me."

The man lifted a questioning brow at her. "Really?"

She tamped down her irritation at Colt. "Yeah. We're looking for Dasha."

"What? You into threesomes?"

Serena shrugged. "Something like that."

"Do you know her?" Colt asked.

The man shrugged. "I've seen her around."

The bartender pushed their beers toward them, and Serena took a sip, her gaze spanning the dark room. A big-haired redhead sidled in from a back entrance, her miniskirt showcasing killer legs, her lips painted to match her hair.

The blonde they'd met outside stood behind her, then gestured toward Colt.

"Dasha's here." Serena wiped her mouth with the back of her hand and sashayed across the room past the pool table and two husky men wearing painters' clothes parked in a booth wolfing down burgers.

The blonde scooted out the door, and Dasha sashayed to the corner near the restroom, pulled out a cigarette and lit up. Serena ignored the curious looks of the in-ebriated men as she ducked past the dart game and met the redhead.

Colt propped himself against the wall casually. "You're Dasha?"

The redhead tilted her head back and blew a string of smoke into the air. "Who wants to know?"

"My name is Serena Stover," Serena said, and Dasha instantly stiffened.

"You're Parker's wife," Dasha said more in acknowledgment than a question. She glanced away, tapped the ashes from the cigarette onto the scarred wooden floor, then sighed. "Some sad crap, him gettin' blown away like that. He was a decent man."

Serena's stomach clenched. She'd had so many mixed feelings about Parker the past two years, that it surprised her to hear this woman's thoughts. Then again, even if Parker hadn't slept with Dasha, the woman could have been in love with him.

What did it matter now?

"Dasha, I need your help," Serena said, hoping to relate as one woman to another. Maybe two women who had loved the same man.

Dasha studied Serena, then cut her gaze toward Colt. "And you? What do you want out of this?"

"Just answers," Colt said, then removed two fifties from his wallet and pushed them into Dasha's hand. "I guess you haven't seen the news?"

Dasha shrugged. "TV don't work. What's goin' on?"

"I was arrested for killing a man named Lyle Rice," Serena said.

"Why'd you kill him?" Dasha stiffened her spine. "He get mean with you?"

Serena bit her lip. "I barely knew the man. I'd met him for coffee then had dinner, but he hit my son so I told him to get out. That night he was supposedly murdered." Serena shuddered as the vile memory intruded on her calm. "Anyway, I was framed. But the short story is that social services took my son, but he was kidnapped that night. I'm looking for him now."

Dasha inhaled another drag of her cigarette. "What makes you think I know something about your boy?"

"Listen, Dasha," Colt said, his voice laced with impatience. "So far we know Parker Stover was working undercover, and that his investigation got him killed. We also know Rice had a vendetta against Stover because he arrested him."

"And," Serena said, her voice brittle, "I talked to Parker's partner and he admitted you were Parker's CI."

A look of panic streaked Dasha's green eyes, making her look pale even in the dark. She tapped her cigarette, then raised a finger to her mouth to shush them as the pool player who'd looked at Serena lumbered by and strode into the john.

"You don't go sayin' that out loud," Dasha muttered. "Next thing you know I be six feet under."

Serena caught Dasha's arm. "Look, Dasha, I don't care what kind of relationship you had with my husband. I honestly don't. All I want is to find Petey." She lowered her voice, tried to appeal to the woman's maternal instincts, and wondered if she possessed that side at all.

Tears blurred Dasha's eyes for a moment, then she tossed the cigarette to the floor and crushed it with her boot. "I'm sorry about your kid, I really am."

"Then tell us what you know," Colt demanded.

The pool guy exited the bathroom, shot Dasha a dark look, then meandered back to the pool table. A chill skated up Serena's spine. Had he been listening to their conversation?

Dasha seemed panicked, swung away and quickly veered into the bathroom. Serena followed her, and caught her just before she disappeared into a stall.

"You're gonna get me killed just like Parker," Dasha bit out.

Serena ignored the jab of guilt that comment triggered. "I'm sorry, Dasha, but my son is only six, and I'm terrified that he might be hurt. The kidnapper hasn't phoned for a ransom, and I don't know where else to turn. Just tell me what Parker was investigating. Was it a drug ring? Something else?"

Dasha flinched as if Serena's statement troubled her, then released a heartfelt labored sigh. "It wasn't drugs," Dasha murmured, giving her a sympathetic look.

Serena didn't want her sympathy. "If not drugs, then what?"

A pained look stretched across Dasha's face. "It was a child kidnapping ring."

PETEY WOKE TO THE SOUND of crying.

He was curled on his side, his hands and feet tied, but the rag around his eyes was gone.

Still, it was so dark he couldn't see his own fingers or where he was. His body bounced and slammed into a metal wall. The rumbling of an engine, of cars passing by, of the gears grinding echoed in his head.

A truck. He must be in the back of some kind of truck. It hit a rough patch and he bounced again, then tires screeched as the vehicle veered sideways, throwing him to the opposite wall.

The sob grew louder.

"Help me," a voice whispered into the dark. "Please, is someone there?"

Petey swallowed against the vile taste of whatever the man had drugged him with. He was so thirsty he could hardly make his voice work.

But he had to.

The sound was a little girl. She must be tied up just like him.

A low wail rent the air, and then the sound of finger-nails scratching against the metal wall. "Let me out," the little girl cried.

"Me, too."

Petey froze. Another little girl was in here, too.

Petey tried to crawl toward them. He didn't know why the man had locked them in here or ripped him from bed. He didn't know where his mommy was, but she'd answered the phone so she must be out of jail.

The sobbing continued, and he blinked back his own tears and moved toward the sound. The truck bounced again, throwing him sideways, and his shoulder hit the wall. But a second later, he careened to the other side.

"I know someone's here," the little girl cried. "Who are you?"

Petey sucked back a cry himself, then rolled toward her. "I'm Petey," he whispered.

"Did the mean man steal you, too?" the other little girl whispered.

"Yes." He scooted closer to them and felt both little

girls shaking. "Shh, don't cry," he murmured. "Everything's gonna be all right. I'll 'tect you."

Then he closed his eyes and pictured his mommy and Mr. Colt in his mind. Mr. Colt would find them. He was smart and big and strong, and Petey had hired him so he wouldn't give up. And as soon as he got a chance, he'd blow that whistle Mr. Colt gave him.

Then someone would find them and call their mommies and they could go home.

Chapter Eleven

"A child kidnapping ring?" Serena whispered. "In North Carolina?"

Dasha shrugged. "Look, that's all I know. Parker never meant to tell me that much. It just sort of slipped out when…" She paused, her eyes widening as if she realized she'd said too much.

"When you were in bed," Serena said, realizing her first instincts had been correct.

Dasha jerked her head downward and spoke beneath her breath. "He still loved you, you know. He just… The undercover work got to him sometimes."

"And you understood that," Serena said.

As if she hadn't grown up on the streets and would have understood, too. Only she had shut down that part of her life and refused to share it with him.

So he'd done the same.

"What else do you know about this kidnapping ring?" Serena asked. "Was Rice part of it?"

Dasha's earrings jangled as she shrugged. "I told you, that's all I know. Now, I need to get back to work before someone gets suspicious."

She pushed past Serena out the door, leaving the cheap scent of her perfume and more questions lingering behind.

Perspiration beaded on Serena's neck, and she splashed water on her face, then grabbed a paper towel and patted her cheeks dry. Her pulse pounded as she rushed out the bathroom door. She spotted Dasha near the back entrance having a heated discussion with the pool boy, but she raced to Colt.

"What did she tell you?" Colt asked.

Serena's throat felt thick. "Parker thought he'd stumbled onto a child kidnapping ring."

Colt muttered an obscenity. "Did she say who's behind it?"

Serena shook her head. "She didn't know any details. But Colt, if Petey was abducted as part of a kidnapping ring, then whoever took him doesn't plan to give him back."

The horror stories on the news about abducted kids being sold to strangers as sex slaves and being shipped to foreign countries never to be seen again bombarded her, and pure terror threatened to bring her to her knees.

COLT GRIPPED HIS HANDS into fists, struggling to control his own reaction. Petey had come to him for help, and he'd let him down.

Had Parker really discovered a child kidnapping ring? If so and the man who'd abducted Petey was involved, then Petey was in grave danger.

Cissy's comment about sensing that other kids had been tied in the same truck she had been locked in reverberated in his head. Dear God. Pedderson hadn't only taken Cissy for his sister as they'd originally thought, but he'd known Rice, and might have been connected to a child kidnapping ring.

Alarm bolted through him. But whom were they selling the kids to? People wanting to adopt? Child predators? Human trafficking rings?

"Come on." He gestured for Serena to follow him, and they maneuvered through the bar and outside. As soon as they settled inside his SUV, Colt punched in the number for GAI. "Gage, it's Colt. There's been a development. Can you put Ben on speakerphone?"

"Sure, hang on a second."

Colt waited until Ben came on the line. "What's up?"

Colt gripped his phone as he sped from the parking lot. "Serena and I just met with Parker Stover's CI. Stover was investigating a child kidnapping ring. We think that's what got him killed, and that the person behind it abducted Petey."

"Dammit," Gage muttered. "Then Cissy's comments make sense. Pedderson must have been involved."

"Yeah, push Mansfield hard, and see if he knows who's behind the deal," Colt said.

"I will. And I'm calling my friend Agent Metcalf at the Bureau. Maybe he's gotten wind of this ring and can fill us in."

Ben cleared his throat. "The code in the ledger could have been dates of kidnappings or drops, even business transactions. Let me take a crack at it from that angle and see if I can pinpoint details of the abductions. Maybe cracking the code will reveal where they're taking the kids."

Serena shivered beside him and fresh guilt assaulted Colt. "Maybe Parker was getting too close, and Rice hired Rouse to kill him before he could break up the ring."

"Speaking of Rice," Gage said. "The crime tech called about the blood at Rice's. You were right. A small portion of it was Rice's, but the larger quantity came from an animal. A goat, to be exact."

"So Rice very well may have faked his own death to frame Serena, and then kidnap Petey," Colt said, thinking out loud.

"The evidence definitely points in that direction," Gage said.

Colt glanced at Serena, grimacing at the strain on her face. She'd been tough as nails in that bar, but the realization that some maniac might be planning to sell her son had to be paralyzing her with fear. "We have to find this son of a bitch and nail him," Colt said between gritted teeth.

"The tip hotline is up and running, and I'll contact NCMEC," Gage said. "Maybe something will come in soon."

"Make sure the airport security, train stations and bus stations are also alerted. We don't want Rice getting out of the country."

"I'll get on it right away," Ben said.

Colt struggled to maintain a calm voice. "I have a contact with Special Victims Unit in Raleigh. Maybe he's heard something about this kidnapping ring."

They agreed to keep in touch, and Colt punched Detective Ian Shaw's number. Serena had turned to look out the window, a faint sliver of moonlight streaking her gaunt face. Thick trees and mountains rose around them, ominous, eerily quiet. So many places for a criminal to hide.

Shaw's phone rang once, twice, three, four times, then on the fifth the message machine clicked on. "Shaw, it's Colt. I'm working an investigation regarding a child kidnapping ring. Call me ASAP."

He disconnected and glanced at Serena again. She'd been strong so far, but he sensed the deep pain and fear racking her body, and he ached for her.

His phone trilled, and he figured it was Shaw, but he checked the caller ID again and it was Derrick. "Yeah?"

"Colt, Gage just filled me in on what's happening. Forensics just called. The partial print they found on Derrick's window definitely belonged to Rice. And the boots matched the prints in the dirt outside my window."

"So the bastard is really alive."

"Yeah. Gage and I talked. He's going to call the media and have them rerun the story, alerting everyone that Rice may have Petey."

"Thanks. I'll call Serena's lawyer and see if she can get the charges dropped against Serena."

Serena was watching him quietly as he ended the call. "Lyle is alive?"

He nodded and explained about the prints. "Kay Krantz should be able to get the judge to drop the charges against you now."

She shrugged as if it didn't matter, and he realized that nothing mattered to her now except finding her son.

SERENA'S CHEST CLENCHED, despair threatening. But she couldn't give up yet.

Colt covered her hand with his. "We will find him, Serena. And when we do, you want to be free so you can both put this nightmare behind you."

Serena nodded, yet a cold knot of grief and fear twisted her gut. She wasn't sure she could survive without her son.

Resorting to self-preservation mode, she closed her eyes, desperate to block out the terrifying images of what her son might be facing. But the sound of her son's cries couldn't be silenced.

The lull of the vehicle grinding gears and coasting around the mountain finally dulled her senses, though, and she drifted asleep. Oblivion would have been a reprieve, but even in her sleep, the nightmares tormented her.

She jerked awake just as Colt pulled into the driveway. Darkness coated the house, only a thin thread of light streaking the front window where her son usually slept.

The silence in the house sent a wave of pain through her as they entered. It had been twenty-four hours since Petey had gone missing.

When she'd heard the news she'd been terrified, but had hoped to trade him for ransom money.

Now she realized that ransom wasn't the motive.

It was much worse. Rice was going to sell her son on the streets, maybe in some foreign country, where kids became lost forever.

Colt moved up behind her, and rubbed her arms. "I know it's hard, Serena, but try to stay positive. We will arrest this ring and find Petey."

Colt's caring concern brought tears to her eyes, and she leaned against him, desperately needing his comforting voice and arms.

She slid her hands up his torso and rubbed slow circles across his chest. His breath hitched slightly, and he wrapped his arms around her and cradled her against him.

"I know it's been a rough day," he murmured against her hair.

"I just want my son back," she whispered.

"I know, and we will get him back." He pressed a gentle kiss on her forehead and the tears began to slip down her cheeks. But he didn't push for more. Instead, he held her and let her vent her emotions until she finally sighed and wiped at her face.

Then she tilted her head back and looked into his eyes. He'd driven all night and looked tired, but compassion and concern and other emotions she didn't understand registered on his face as if fatigue never slowed him down. With one thumb, he swept her hair away from her forehead. His lips parted, the whisper of his breath brushed her face.

She moaned, part pain, part need. And desire flickered in his eyes. "Serena?"

"Please kiss me, Colt. Make the pain go away for a while."

He clenched his jaw. "I don't want to take advantage of you."

She traced a finger along his taut cheek. "It's not taking advantage if I ask."

He stared at her for another long moment, indecision warring with raw hunger on his face. Then he lowered his mouth and settled his mouth over hers. Eager for his warmth, she parted her lips and savored his touch as their mouths melded together.

She was hungry, needy, yearning for something that seemed beyond her reach. Desperate to forget that her son was missing, that her husband had slept with his CI, that Lyle Rice had used her for his revenge.

That desperation drove her to plunge her tongue into Colt's mouth, to take as well as receive, to strip his shirt and trace her fingers over the soft whorls of dark hair covering his broad chest.

Parker had been strong and muscular but lean compared to Colt's rock-hard body. His breath caught again, and he traced his lips along her jaw, suckling the sensitive skin behind her ear and trailing kisses along her neck until his fingers began to shove at her T-shirt.

She raised her arms, inviting him to strip the shirt, and he did. A cool breeze from the air conditioner sent a shiver through her, or maybe it was the passionate look of appreciation in his eyes as he skimmed his gaze over her lacy black bra.

She had an affinity for sheer undergarments and the

bra hid nothing from his perusal. Instead, her nipples jutted and strained against the sheer fabric, begging for his hands and mouth.

THE SIGHT OF SERENA in that lacy black bra triggered a fever inside Colt. He had never seen anything more beautiful.

His chest was tingling from her touch, his lips aching to close themselves over one turgid nipple and tug it into his mouth.

She licked her lips and emitted a low moan of pleasure as if she enjoyed his visual perusal. Hungry for more, he pulled her against him, and the friction of their bodies rubbing together stirred his primal instincts.

He hadn't been with a woman in ages. For the past two years he felt as if his hands held the stench of blood and dirt and lies from his undercover work, that he didn't deserve love or tenderness, at least not from a decent woman.

Maybe that was the reason her husband had hooked up with Dasha. Even if Geoff Harbison denied Parker and Dasha were lovers, Colt had seen the flicker of grief in Dasha's eyes and known Stover's partner had lied. He'd probably wanted to protect Serena.

But Serena was no one's fool.

Anyone could understand the attraction.

Especially a man. Dasha had no expectations, no emotional ties to him. A man could have mindless sex and purge his anxiety without revealing the pain he carried inside or his own needs.

A man could not do that with Serena.

His heart pounded. He was getting too close to her. Caring about her. Caring about her son. For that very reason, the rational voice insides his head ordered him to stop.

But his hands disobeyed and inched themselves along Serena's spine, urging her nearer. She threaded her fingers in his hair and traced her tongue along his nipple, and he sucked in a raspy breath.

Dammit, how could he pull away when he wanted her with every fiber of his being?

He plunged his tongue into the warm cavern of her mouth again and ravaged her with his kiss, hungry, needy, anxious to make her forget her fear, if only for a moment. Her hands urged him to take her, and he lowered his mouth and nibbled at her throat and neck, until he reached the lacy rim of her bra. He tugged it away with his teeth, and suckled the soft skin beneath, then flipped open the front clasp of her bra.

Her lush breasts fell into his waiting hands, and he massaged them gently, tracing his fingers over her jutting nipples. She moaned again, and he licked his way to one stiff peak and drew it into his mouth.

She sighed with pleasure, stroking his calf with her foot as he laved one breast then the other. Spurned by her excitement, he yanked her hips into his and rubbed his erection between her thighs.

When she reached for his belt, he moaned in anticipation and unsnapped her jeans.

But the jangle of the telephone cut into the moment, and both of them froze. His ragged breathing punctuated the silence, and they stared at each other for a brief second. The desire and need in her eyes wrenched his gut. He wanted to pleasure her more than he wanted his next breath.

But fear also registered, and so did reality, and he moved away, grabbed his phone, and hit the connect button.

"Colt," Derrick said, "we released the news that Rice might be alive along with his and Petey's photo, and we just received a call on the tip line."

The hope in Derrick's voice shocked him into an adrenaline rush. "What did the caller say?"

"The man runs a gas station in Savannah, Georgia. Said he saw Rice and Petey a few minutes ago."

"Did Ben find anything connecting Rice to Savannah? Family or an old girlfriend?"

"No. Nothing."

Then why Savannah? Because it was a port?

Colt reached for his jeans. "I'm going to Savannah."

"Ben will book flights for you and Serena and reserve a rental car."

"Thanks."

Hope warred with fear as Colt ended the call. Savannah was too near the coast for comfort.

If Rice put Petey on a ship, they could disappear anywhere in the Atlantic.

Chapter Twelve

Serena's body still quaked from Colt's touch, but guilt suffused her and she quickly refastened her bra and yanked on her T-shirt. How could she have been kissing Colt, about to make love, when her son was still missing and in danger?

Once again she'd been selfish.

"Serena, that was Derrick," Colt said. "Someone in Savannah, Georgia, spotted Rice with Petey."

Serena's chest clenched. "So Petey is still alive?"

Colt nodded. "And we were right about Rice. He staged his own death and framed you, then kidnapped Petey."

A shudder rippled through Serena. How could she ever have thought she might be interested in Lyle? He was a monster. "He's going to sell Petey to get back at Parker for almost destroying his operation."

"It looks that way." Colt grabbed his shirt from the floor and stuffed his arms into the sleeves, and Serena couldn't help but watch. His muscles were so strong and powerful, his biceps flexing and straining.

Yet he'd been so gentle and loving when he'd held her that she'd lost all rational thought.

"If you want to stay here and rest, I'll call you and keep you updated," Colt offered.

Serena shook her head. "No, let me pack an overnight bag. When we find Petey, I want to be there."

She had to. She needed to take him in her arms and assure him that he was safe, that she'd never let anyone hurt him again.

Anxious to get on the road, she raced to her room, retrieved her overnight bag from the closet and started tossing clothes inside. An extra pair of jeans, three shirts, socks, underwear, tennis shoes, then her toiletries. Within five minutes, she ran back into the den, snatched her denim jacket, purse and phone and was ready to go.

Colt took her bag. "On the way, I'll phone the Savannah P.D. and inform them Rice has been spotted and phone the sherriff. Maybe they'll find him before we arrive."

Serena nodded, and he punched in Gage's number as they hurried to his SUV. But as she listened to Colt talk to the sheriff, she wondered why Rice had taken Petey to Savannah.

And where he might go from there.

"THANK YOU, Sergeant Black," Colt said. "We appreciate the Savannah P.D.'s cooperation."

"No problem. We'll do everything we can to find this child and see that justice is done."

By the time they arrived at the airport in Asheville,

Ben had emailed Colt their itinerary. They caught the first flight out, flew through Charlotte and on to Atlanta. Colt tried to grab a few winks on the plane ride, but adrenaline kept him from falling into a deep sleep.

Rice was already miles and hours ahead of them. By now, he could have long left Savannah and be God knows where.

The hour layover in Atlanta gave them just enough time to hit a coffee shop and wolf down a muffin. Serena stared out the window as another plane coasted down the runway. "Petey must be so scared," she said in a pained voice. "Where do you think Rice is taking him?"

Colt didn't want to speculate. Any ideas he had would only magnify Serena's fears. "Maybe this witness can give us a lead."

The flight attendant announced they were ready to board, so they tossed their trash into the bin, then headed to the gate. A strained silence fell over them as they claimed their seats and the plane departed.

Two rows in front of them, a woman with three boys tried to corral their boisterous behavior while the lady in the seat across from them cradled a baby girl to her chest.

Colt saw Serena watching them with envy and the affectionate look of a mother who understood the problems associated with children, but one who adored them anyway.

"Sometimes we take our families for granted until they're gone," she said softly.

"I doubt you ever took Petey for granted, Serena. You're a wonderful mother."

"But I didn't keep him safe, did it? I was foolish enough to believe Lyle Rice wasn't dangerous when he was only using me."

Colt frowned and slid his arm around her. "Unfortunately we can do everything possible to protect our children, but it's not always enough. Bad things just happen."

"You sound like you're talking from experience."

Colt chewed the inside of his cheek. He rarely talked about his past, but he decided to share now. Anything to help assuage her guilt.

"My younger brother was killed when he was twelve," he said. "I was home watching him, and let him have a friend over."

"What happened?" Serena asked.

Colt swallowed, the memory so fresh and raw it was as if it happened yesterday, not fifteen years ago.

"His friend snuck in a gun. His dad's .45. I was on the phone when I heard the shot go off."

Sympathy mingled with horror on Serena's face. "Oh, my God."

Sweat broke out on Colt's neck. "I ran in and tried to save him, but he died in my arms."

"I'm so sorry, Colt," Serena said. "That's so sad."

Colt nodded, the old familiar guilt raging through him. "It tore my mother apart. We'd just lost my dad, and she counted on me, then I let her down." He swallowed against the emotions in his throat. "And the other boy…he was so riddled with guilt he turned to drugs. Last I heard he'd been in and out of rehab."

Serena sighed. "I don't think I could survive if we don't find Petey."

Colt pulled her closer to him, and she buried her head against his shoulder. She was stronger than she thought, but he was determined she wouldn't have to face life without her son.

Still, he understood her fear.

His brother's death was the sole reason he'd specialized in guns and worked to clean up the streets. But each time he'd put one away, another cropped up.

Serena's husband must have felt the same way about drugs.

But then he'd stumbled onto a child kidnapping ring and now his own family was being destroyed because of it.

Colt silently vowed to find Petey and abolish that ring so others like Petey wouldn't suffer.

Serena nestled against him, and he closed his eyes. For a brief moment he allowed himself to believe that once her son was home safe, and he disbanded this kidnapping ring, they might have a future together.

But the sound of the engine rumbling jarred him back to reality. Serena and Petey were a family. He was not a part of it.

His life revolved around work. Moving from one case to the next.

The team at GAI was all the family he would ever have.

SERENA STRUGGLED to remain positive as they departed the plane in Savannah and Colt rented a car. Derrick had texted him the address of the gas station where Petey and Rice had been spotted the night before.

Colt plugged the address into the GPS monitor, exited the airport and made his way onto 95. Signs for hotels and tourist sights in Savannah sprang up. Billboards of carriage rides, ghost tours, restaurants, antebellum homes, shopping, voodoo shops and the riverfront looked inviting, but the idea of the cemetery tour unnerved her.

"Why would he bring Petey here?" Serena asked.

Colt shrugged, his face stony. "I don't know. It may or may not be his intended destination."

Serena considered the airport, the islands off the coast, and the port, and fear seized her again. Rice was hours ahead of them. "Do you think Rice is planning to ship Petey away or sell him?"

Colt scrubbed a hand through his hair. "Let's not go there," he said. "We have leads now. We're closing in."

But Serena had seen the dregs of society. And if Rice didn't plan to sell Petey, if he killed him, Rice could dump his body in the ocean, and they might never find him…

Colt veered off the exit, sped down the ramp and turned right. The bright lights of a motel gleamed against the sky, blinking like cheap Christmas lights. Beside it stood the gas station.

Colt swung the sedan into the parking lot, and they climbed out and went inside. Sunshine slanted rays across the asphalt, breaking through the clouds, and heating up the day. The scent of gasoline and oil hung in the air along with the aroma of French fries and burgers flowing from the attached fast food restaurant.

A big black pot in a corner of the parking lot bubbled with steam, a hand-painted sign made of cardboard boasting boiled peanuts for sale. A small fruit and vegetable stand sat beside it, under the watchful eye of an ancient-looking woman with leathery skin wearing a bonnet selling apples, fresh tomatoes, green beans, squash and potatoes in small cardboard containers.

"I'll talk to the clerk inside. You want to ask the woman what she saw?" Colt suggested.

Serena nodded, walked over to the vendor, introduced herself and showed her a picture of Petey. "Someone from this station phoned yesterday saying they spotted a man with my son."

The woman squinted up at her. "Yeah, I seen you on the news. Sorry about your boy."

"Did you see Rice and my son here?" Serena asked.

The woman shook her head. "Afraid not. I took sick yesterday with my arthritis, and had to shut down the stand."

Disappointment ballooned in Serena's chest. "Well, thanks anyway."

"I sure hope you find him," the woman called.

Serena nodded and crossed the parking lot to the store. When she entered, Colt was talking to a white-haired man behind the counter. She glanced around for other patrons, but the station was empty.

"Yeah, I was the one who called that tip line," the man said. "Man in that picture on the news, he was here all right."

Serena sucked in a sharp breath, then handed him her son's photograph. "Was this little boy with him?"

The man's hands shook slightly as he took the picture and studied it. "Yeah, that was the boy. He had on a baseball hat, though, a little too big for him I thought, and held his head down low. At first, I didn't think nothing of it. But the man kept a hand on his shoulder the whole time, kept him right up next to him."

"So he wouldn't try to escape or ask for help," Colt muttered.

"Was he okay?" Serena asked. "He didn't look hurt?"

Sympathy flickered in the man's eyes. "Didn't see no bruises, if that's what you mean. But…right before they left, the boy looked up at me. And I saw it in his eyes."

Serena's heart pounded. "What did you see?"

"The fear. Course I just figured he was scared of his old man, that he was in trouble for some reason." The old man wheezed. "But this morning when I saw that news story and the picture of your boy and that criminal, that's when I put two and two together and called the tip line."

"We appreciate your help," Colt said. "Did Rice say anything about where he might be going?"

The old man shook his head. "Didn't say much. Just

paid for his gas, bought some burgers and fries, and left."

"What was he driving?" Colt asked.

"A white van, you know one of them utility kind."

"Was there a logo on the side?"

"No. Didn't see the tag either." He made a face. "Sorry."

Colt propped his hip against the counter. "Is there anything else you remember?"

The man pulled his hand down his chin in thought, then snapped his fingers. "Oh, yeah. He had a map of Florida he was looking at while the boy was in the john. Circled Miami with a red marker."

Serena's lungs tightened. Miami. He was taking Petey farther and farther away from her.

"Did you see which direction he went when he left?" Colt asked.

"He drove over to that motel across the street."

Serena's heart clamored. "Colt, maybe they're still there."

Colt took her hand and they jogged to the car. Serena swallowed hard as they crossed the street.

COLT FORCED HIMSELF to keep the panic off his face as he and Serena drove across the street to the hotel. If Rice was on his way to Miami and involved in a kidnapping ring, then Petey was in terrible danger. Putting Petey on a ship that sailed out of the country would make it almost impossible to track him down.

Colt parked at the motel, swiping perspiration from

his brow as he and Serena entered the front doors. The July heat had kicked in, temperature soaring, and it was muggy, mosquitoes buzzing through the air.

A young African-American clerk with orange hair and a tattoo stood behind the reception desk. Her name tag read Shanika.

Colt explained who they were and their reason for visiting.

The clerk checked the register. "I'm sorry, sir, but no one by the name of Rice checked in last night."

Of course he wouldn't use his real name. "He goes by various aliases. Let me look at the list."

"We can't do that, sir. It's against our policy."

"To hell with the policy," Serena said sharply. "This maniac kidnapped my son and may have abducted other children. You have to help us."

A pudgy woman wearing a purple knit suit emerged from behind a closed door. "What's going on here?"

Shanika hitched her hip sideways. "These people want to look at the register."

Serena shoved the picture of Petey toward her. "This is my son. You've probably seen the news about his kidnapping."

The woman narrowed her eyes at the photo, then looked back up at Serena. "I saw the man but not the boy. He paid cash. Reeked of fast food and French fries."

Serena paled. "Petey wasn't with him?"

The woman shrugged. "Don't know. He parked the

van in front till he got his key, then drove around back to the room."

"Which room?" Colt asked.

The woman pointed a finger at the register. "Three-eighteen. Specifically requested a room on the back side. Said he needed some sleep, didn't want the sun waking him up."

"That was bull," Colt said. "He didn't want anyone to spot him carrying a kid inside."

Serena gripped the counter. "Is he still there?"

"Left early this morning." The woman turned to Shanika. "You find anything when you cleaned the room?"

Shanika toyed with the gold loops in her ear. "I ain't had time to clean it yet."

The woman glared at Shanika, but snatched the room key. "Come on. You can take a look."

Colt and Serena followed the manager outside and around the back to room 318. Colt scoured the parking lot for the white van, but it hadn't returned. Not a good sign.

The manager twisted the key and started to enter, but Colt signaled her to let him go first, so she stepped aside. The strong odor of cigarette smoke, burgers and French fries filled the room.

He glanced at the beds. Both unmade.

Relief surged through him. At least Rice hadn't used Petey for himself. He glanced at Serena and saw her studying the room, as well.

Colt searched the closet, then the dresser and trash,

looking for anything that Rice might have left behind, hoping that he'd scribbled an address or left some indicator as to his plans.

Serena had stepped inside the bathroom, then she gasped.

His lungs constricted. Dear God, no.

What if Rice had killed Petey and left his body behind?

Chapter Thirteen

Serena stared at the mirror, her heart thumping wildly with fear. The letters on the mirror, the writing, the childlike scrawl, the words…

Help me.

Was it written in blood?

She trembled all over, knowing she needed to touch it to know, but denial forced her hands to her sides, and she began to pray with all her might, just as she'd prayed for help when she'd been stuck in those awful foster homes and lost on the streets herself.

She'd never wanted Petey to suffer as she had.

And now he was with some maniac who had evil purposes in mind. Had Petey fought him? Had he tried to escape and Rice punished him by hurting him?

She lifted her finger to touch the message, but Colt rushed in and caught her hand. "Don't touch it, Serena."

A sob caught in her throat. "But Petey wrote it and he's scared, and it looks like he's injured."

Colt inched closer to the mirror and examined the writing. He lifted one finger and dabbed the corner, careful not to damage the imprint, then sniffed it.

A frown marred his face, then he shocked her by touching his finger to his mouth.

"What are you doing?" Serena asked.

Colt sighed. "It's ketchup, Serena." A small grin tugged at his mouth. "Petey wrote the message with ketchup."

Serena's shoulders sagged in relief.

"Everything all right in there?" the manager called.

"Yes," Colt said, then took Serena's hand. "Let's go. We have to catch a flight to Miami."

Colt thanked the manager then phoned GAI to fill them in as he drove toward the airport. Ben booked them a flight and another rental car to be picked up when they arrived in Miami.

Serena's cell phone jangled, and she dug it from her purse, praying it was Petey or Rice, but when she checked the number, it was Kay Krantz.

She punched Connect, hoping the woman didn't have more bad news. Like her bail had been revoked because she'd left the state.

"Hello. This is Serena."

"Serena, it's Kay Krantz. Listen, a bit of good news. I just met with the judge and the sheriff and in light of the forensics and the eyewitness claiming he saw Rice alive, they've dropped the charges against you. Congratulations. You're a free woman."

Serena pressed her hand to her throat. Yes, getting the charges dropped was good news.

But what did it matter if she was free if she didn't find her son?

BY THE TIME COLT and Serena landed in Miami, it was early evening. The sun was fading although the temperature had hit the hundred-plus mark, and the air felt stifling.

Colt quickly commandeered the rental car, fatigue adding to his frustration. He was going on more than twenty-four hours without sleep, but he didn't have time to stop and rest.

Even with Rice driving and them taking flights, the creep could have dropped Petey with someone else and be headed to his own destination to hide out.

His cell phone buzzed just as he and Serena pulled away from the airport. It was Ian Shaw from the Special Victims Unit. "Ian?"

"Yeah. I got your message, and I've seen the reports on the missing boy. You think his disappearance is connected to a child kidnapping ring?"

"It looks that way. The boy's father was a cop who was killed working undercover. His CI claimed he had a lead on a kidnapping ring. We think that's what got him killed."

Ian made a sound of disgust in his throat. "And Lyle Rice is involved?"

"Yes. Parker Stover arrested him, so I think he abducted Stover's son for revenge."

"About Rice," Ian said. "I recognized one of his old aliases. We have two missing child cases here in Raleigh. Both girls are age six, brown hair, brown eyes. The first girl is Kinsey Jones, the second Ellie Pinkerton. They were kidnapped within a few hours of each other, and both attended the same elementary school."

"When were they kidnapped?"

"Ten days ago. Kinsey's mother recognized Rice from one of the shots on the news. She's a real-estate broker, said she showed him some property. He claimed he had children and wanted to see the elementary school, as well."

"He was casing her family and the school."

"It appears that way. If you find him, he might have both girls."

Dammit. "No telling how many kids are involved," Colt said. "Email me the girls' photos and information and I'll keep you posted."

When Colt ended the call, he headed toward the local police department.

"What was that about?" Serena asked.

"My friend with the SVU in Raleigh. Two little girls were kidnapped there ten days ago. One of the mothers recognized Rice's photo. He was casing the elementary school."

"So Petey wasn't his only victim." A shudder coursed through Serena. "How could someone steal innocent children and sell them like they're property?"

"He's sick and depraved," Colt said. "But he's not going to get away with it, Serena."

She turned to look out the window, and Colt noted the swaying palm trees, the rippling tides of the ocean, and beach properties, a dramatic change from the mountains. Miami was a happening city, a virtual resort for families and young people who enjoyed the nightlife. Celebrities also flocked to the town for its beauty, private island resorts and recreational resources.

Yet crime thrived, the waterways providing an escape for drug runners, illegal aliens, and other corrupt business ventures—like trading and selling children.

Five minutes later, he parked at the Miami-Dade County Police Department (MDPD), and he and Serena went inside. A lean dark-skinned Cuban man, Sergeant Cal Sanchez, escorted them into his office, and Colt caught him up on his investigation.

"Do you have any leads on a child kidnapping ring?" Colt asked.

Sergeant Sanchez rubbed a hand over his shaved head. "No, but I'll talk to my undercover agents and have them dig around. If this bastard is using our city for human trafficking, we have to stop him."

"Please post the photos of Rice and Petey Stover for your men. I'll forward you photos of two missing little girls from Raleigh, North Carolina, who we suspect Rice abducted, too." Colt paused. "He was casing schools and was last seen driving a plain white van, so he may have more children locked inside." Colt accessed his email on his phone and forwarded the photos.

"I'll have my men check out boating docks, abandoned properties, and put feelers out on the streets."

Colt battled disgust. "He approached the mother of the Raleigh child and asked her to show him property. Maybe he's doing the same here. Or he could be holed up in an empty rental."

"With the market tanking, there are dozens of those." Sergeant Sanchez stood. "But I'll put some officers on that angle ASAP."

Although Colt doubted Rice planned to stick around.

He knew the police were onto him, and he'd be looking to run. "The airports, train and bus stations have been alerted, but you could help us by alerting port authorities here in Miami," Colt said.

"Of course," Sanchez agreed.

Colt thanked him and placed his hand on the small of Serena's back as they left. As soon as they stepped onto the pavement, the sweltering heat assaulted them, nearly robbing him of breath.

"Where to now?" Serena asked. "They could be anywhere. Rice could have Petey on a ship by now and be leaving Florida—"

"Don't," Colt said. "Agents and cops nationwide are looking for him." They climbed back in the rental car and he drove through downtown Miami. "Let me check in with Gage."

Serena nodded and folded her arms, visually scanning the streets as tourists and families strolled by, and he realized she was searching for Petey in the crowd.

Gage answered on the first ring. "Colt, are you in Miami now?"

"Yes. We just talked with a sergeant at MDPD."

"Good. Special Agent Mitchell Metcalf is flying out from Quantico. He'll meet up with you there."

"Fine. Any information from Mansfield?"

"He denies knowing anything about a major kidnapping ring."

Same old song and dance he'd given since Dr. Emery's arrest.

"But Ben may have something. I'm putting you on speaker."

Colt waited a second and heard Ben murmur something to Gage. "Colt. I did some more digging around on Rice and discovered two things. One of his former cell mates has skipped out on his probation and may be helping him. And two, he has his pilot's license."

Colt tensed. "Dammit. There are several private airports around Miami."

"Exactly. And some of the islands have areas large enough for landing a small plane."

He hated to voice his fears out loud, but he and Ben were on the same wavelength. Rice might be planning to fly Petey out of the country in a private jet.

He'd check the ones nearest the city first. "Do you have directions to the private airports nearest Miami?"

"I'm texting them to you now."

Colt thanked Ben and disconnected. When he turned to Serena, her face looked ashen. "Oh, God, Colt. Tell me he hasn't already left the country with Petey."

He wished to hell he could.

Colt swallowed hard and spun the car around, heading back to 95. The tires screeched on the sedan as he accelerated and sped toward the nearest private airport.

SERENA CLENCHED the armrest, her pulse racing as she fought the images bombarding her, but she'd seen news stories about human trafficking and the images assaulted her anyway. Petey and other children locked in the back of that van in the oppressive heat. Or Petey tied and bound and tossed on a plane like some kind of cargo that Rice planned to sell.

Colt veered off 95 and they traveled another ten miles, the more populated area turning to marshland. A private jet zoomed overhead and she stared up at it, wondering if that very plane might be carrying her son away.

Colt turned down the long drive to the airport, bypassing palm trees and grassland, and ahead she spotted the airport. A long rectangular building looked as if it served as the terminal, a parking lot held a handful of vehicles, and several hangars were spread out behind the main terminal.

No white van.

Although a small black cargo van sporting a logo for pool supplies sat near one of the hangars.

Colt pulled up in front of the airport and parked, and they walked up to the entrance, both of them scanning the perimeter in case Rice or his accomplice was there, but the place seemed virtually deserted.

Colt squeezed her arm. "You okay?"

Serena frowned. "I won't be okay until we find my son."

Colt nodded, his eyes worried, then pushed open the door. The inside of the airport resembled a commercial terminal but on a much smaller scale. Seating areas were scattered throughout, along with restrooms; there was a small store, which had a closed sign on it, and an information desk had been carved in the center.

A thin gray-haired man wearing a dark blue security uniform sat at the desk, his boots on the top, his head lolled back, his mouth slack, snoring.

Colt strode toward him and rapped his knuckles on the desk. Serena read his name tag—Homer.

"Hey, Homer," Colt said. "We need your help."

The old man jerked awake, then rubbed his blurry eyes. "What? You need to charter a plane?"

"No," Colt said. "We need information."

Serena removed the photos of Rice and Petey from her purse and laid them on the desk while Colt explained about their search.

"The man we're looking for, Lyle Rice, has a pilot's license," Colt said. "We think he may be planning to transport Ms. Stover's son and possibly other kidnapped children out of the country. Have you seen him?"

The man leaned forward, his frown deepening the grooves around his mouth and eyes. "No, can't say as I have."

"He was last seen driving a white van," Colt said. "Have you seen it parked here?"

Homer scratched his chin. "Hmm, no, sure haven't. But I've been inside all day and my eyes ain't what they used to be."

"Show me your flight log," Colt demanded.

Homer shoved a clipboard toward him, and Colt studied the manifest. Nothing there except for one scheduled plane belonging to a woman.

"Who was flying that plane that took off a few minutes ago?" Serena asked.

Homer grinned toothily. "Ansley Freeworth. She just got her pilot's license and wanted to take out her bird."

"Did she have anyone with her?"

"Just her current boy wonder," Homer's tone turned derisive. "She's a rich daddy's girl and has a new one every time she comes."

"So she wasn't transporting any cargo or other passengers?" Colt asked.

"No passengers. Probably a bottle of vodka for her picnic when she lands though."

Serena's chest clenched. She'd hoped Homer could tell them more.

Colt cleared his throat. "Do you mind if we look around outside?"

Homer shrugged his bony shoulders. "Suit yourself."

Colt laid a business card on the desk. "Call me if Rice shows up."

Homer nodded, and Colt led Serena outside. Colt gestured toward the hangars. "Let's check them out. Just because Homer didn't see anything doesn't mean Rice or his accomplice didn't stop by."

Colt headed toward the black van, and Serena rushed to keep up with him. The sun was fading now, night falling, although the heat still felt oppressive. The scent of machine oil and dirt rose to greet her as they approached the van near the hangar.

Colt peered inside the front, and Serena scanned the interior, as well. Nothing. Colt opened the door, and the strong odor of pool chemicals filled the air.

Then suddenly a gunshot rang out.

Serena screamed, and Colt shoved her down behind the van. "Keep low," Colt shouted.

Another shot pinged off the top of the van, then the sound of gravel crunching as footsteps raced across the lot. Serena peered around the van and spotted a chunky man with tattoos up and down his arms running toward a black sedan.

Colt must have seen him, too. He removed his weapon and discharged a bullet, then the man spun around and fired back. The bullet skimmed the top of the front of the van and whizzed over Serena's head.

Then the man dove into the sedan and cranked the engine.

"Stay here. I'm going after him," Colt yelled. Without waiting for a response, he jogged to their rental car, jumped in and sped off after the car.

Serena's heart raced, her breathing turning raspy as she watched them disappear. She glanced at the airport expecting Homer to appear but his hearing must have been as bad as his eyesight.

Pushing to her feet, she surveyed the area just in case Rice had been with the shooter and stayed behind. But the runway, the property surrounding the hangars, the parking lot—there was nothing except a strained silence. Not even the wind blowing to stir the hot air. Not a car engine or the motor of a plane.

But a low keening sound broke the silence. Serena froze, stiffening, straining to hear. Had she imagined the sound?

No. The muffled cry rose from the distance. A child's cry.

Her pulse clamored and she ran to the first hangar and rapped on the metal door. "Hello, is someone in there?"

Nothing.

Another sound, something banging against metal, rent the air, and she raced to the second hangar and tried to open the door, but it was chained and locked. "Is someone in there?"

Suddenly the rattling grew louder as if someone was pounding on one of the doors.

Serena raced down the row of hangars, banging on each one, frantic. By the time she reached the fifth one, she was sweating and shaking.

But she knew without a doubt that someone was trapped inside. Maybe her son.

"Petey!" She banged on the door. "If you're in there, make some noise."

Another low wail, then a sob, low and anguished.

Like the other door, this one was locked and chained. She tried to wrench it open, but it wouldn't budge. Panic threatened, but she tamped it down and tried to think.

She spotted a tool shed a few feet from the first hangar and ran to it. Inside various mechanic tools were stacked in tool chests, others mounted on the wall. She grabbed a pair of bolt cutters, ran back to the hangar, hoisted them and snapped the chain in two.

The chain rattled as she yanked it from the door and tossed it to the ground. It was heavy, but adrenaline kicked in, and she shoved open the door and peered inside. Darkness bathed the interior, the scent of grease and dirt mingling with sweat.

"Is someone here?" she said, inching slowly into the dark space.

Movement stirred from the corner, then a low whimper. She slowly moved toward it. "Please don't be scared. I'm here to help you."

Her shoes squeaked on the concrete floor as she inched her way toward the sound. A sliver of moonlight wormed its way through the opened door and cast a slight shimmer across her path.

Two little children were huddled in the corner, clinging to each other, their muffled sobs reverberating through the darkness and tearing at her heart.

"Petey, is that you? Are you all right?"

She reached out and stroked one of the child's backs, and a little girl looked up at her with tear-stained cheeks. The other child was sobbing harder, and Serena realized it was another little girl.

The two girls Colt had said were kidnapped from Raleigh?

Emotions overcame her and tears filled her eyes. These poor little girls had been left in this hot deserted building with no food or water, and another scorching day to face.

"Shh, come here, you're safe now. We'll call your families and tell them to come and get you." She gathered them against her, and both the children collapsed in her arms, sobbing and clinging to her for dear life.

Her heart ached for them and their families, and the trauma they would have to overcome from their ordeal.

But anguish wrenched her heart. Rice had left the girls behind.

So where was her son?

"LET ME GO!" Petey slammed his fists at the big man's shoulders, kicking and screaming with all his might. "I want my mommy!"

"Shut up, kid!" The man threw him to the floor, then ripped a piece of duct tape from the roll at his waist and shoved it over Petey's mouth. He tried to scream again, but the sound died. Still he beat at the man as he jerked his hands and tied them with rope, then his feet.

Then the mean man dragged some kind of sack over his head and Petey fought harder, hating the darkness. He couldn't see. Couldn't breathe. Couldn't tell where the man was carrying him.

Then he heard the sound of water. Ocean waves. A boat's motor rumbling. The man's feet pounded on something that sounded like wood.

A boat dock.

Fear clogged his throat. The man had left the girls in that nasty hot building at the airport. What was he going to do with him?

The swish of the tides against the dock thrashed, and tears ran down Petey's cheeks. Was he going to throw him into the ocean and leave him to die?

Chapter Fourteen

Colt chased the car to 95, then followed him a few miles until the man veered off onto a side road that ran along the coast. The man was flying, hitting one hundred miles an hour, weaving around traffic and nearly sideswiping cars as he passed on the wrong side.

Colt could barely keep up in the rental car, and cursed as a stream of teenagers flooded the streets, jaywalking, others honking horns as they waved to friends.

Traffic thickened, tourists and locals maneuvering toward the nightspots, and he dodged an oncoming Corvette then bore down on the shooter's car.

But the shooter accelerated again, forcing Colt to do the same. He raced across a bridge over the inlet, but an oncoming vehicle decided to pass on the bridge, and slammed into the shooter. The shooter's car skidded and spun, hit the guardrail, slid to the end of the bridge and plunged into the water below.

The oncoming car sped past, two drunken young men screaming out the window and shouting it was party time.

Colt swung the sedan to the side of the road, screeched

to a stop, threw the sedan into Park then jumped out. He jogged to the side of the waterway and peered down, but the shooter's car sank into the churning water. He ran to the edge, searching to see if the man made it out, but he didn't spot him.

Furious that his only lead might be drowning, he tucked his gun and phone into a drain nearby, threw off his shoes and dove into the water. Sirens wailed in the distance, two other cars had stopped, curious spectators peering at the scene.

He swam toward the car, then ducked beneath the water and dove toward the driver's side. The doors were shut, the windows up, water slowly seeping inside.

Colt grimaced. The man from the photo Ben had sent was inside. His head was slumped against the steering wheel, blood swirling around his face, his eyes staring wide open.

Colt tried the door anyway, but it was jammed. He jerked and tugged, but it wouldn't budge. He balled his hand into a fist and tried to break the window, but the force of the water made it harder, and he couldn't crack the glass.

His own lungs ached for air, but he swam to the opposite side and tried the passenger door and window but no luck. Dammit.

Swimming back to the driver's side, he rapped on the glass but the river of blood was so thick now all he saw was the whites of the man's eyes bulging.

He was dead.

Colt silently cursed as he swam to the surface of the water. By the time he reached the bank, two police officers and an ambulance were rushing toward him, and a group of rubberneckers had collected along with a news van and a photographer already snapping shots.

Colt knotted his hands into fists as one of the officers approached.

"Detective Walter Riley, MDPD. Sir, what happened here?"

Colt shook water from his hair, removed his ID from his pocket and explained about his investigation. "You can call Sergeant Sanchez. Ms. Stover and I spoke with him earlier about her son's kidnapping and Lyle Rice, the man who abducted him."

"Was he the man in the car?"

"No. That was James Ladden, Rice's former cell mate. We believe Ladden was Rice's accomplice. He tried to kill me and Ms. Stover at the private airport nearby. I was in pursuit when he careened into the waterway." Colt glanced back at the water. "I tried to rescue him but couldn't open the door. He was dead. Looks like a head injury."

The detective angled his head toward the other cop. "Call a crew to tow the car, and make sure the ME and crime techs are here when he does."

"Copy that." The officer walked away to make the calls.

The detective turned back to Colt. "Stay here while I call Sanchez."

"Sure." While the cops had turned away, he retrieved his weapon and phone. It buzzed the minute he picked it up, and he checked the number. Serena. He connected the call. "Serena?"

"Colt, are you okay?"

"Yes, I chased the shooter but he crashed into the inlet. I'm at the scene with the cops."

"Does he know where Petey is?"

Colt ran a hand through his soggy hair. "I'm sorry, Serena, but he didn't make it."

A heartbeat of strained silence passed.

"Serena?"

"Yes, I'm here," she whispered hoarsely. "After you left, I heard a noise and started checking the hangars."

"You found Rice and Petey?"

"No," Serna said in an anguished voice. "But there were two little girls in the hangar. Kinsey Jones and Ellie Pinkerton. Colt, he just left them there with no food or water. If they'd been locked there in this heat over-night and all day tomorrow, they could have died."

"Are they hurt?"

"Not that I can see, just traumatized. Homer called the paramedics."

"Good."

"One of them said she knew Petey. He was with the girls in the back of the van." Her voice cracked. "But the girls don't know where Rice took him."

Dammit. "Listen, Serena, I know this is frustrating and scary, but just remember that we know Petey's alive. Hang on to that." The sound of her sniffling tore at his heart.

"When will you be back?"

Colt breathed deeply, wanting to be with her now. "I don't know. The detective is verifying my story. Just stay with the girls. I'll phone Gage so he can let the FBI agent know you found them."

Serena disconnected and he punched Gage's number and filled him in.

"I'll contact Agent Metcalf and Detective Shaw. Metcalf should be landing in Miami any minute. I'll have him meet you at the private airport to inform the parents and arrange for the girls to go home."

"Thanks, Gage."

The detective strode toward him, working his jaw, and Colt hung up.

"Sergeant Sanchez confirmed your story. But I'll need your statement and contact information before you leave."

"Certainly." Colt removed a business card and handed it to the officer. "Serena Stover just called. She found two of the children Rice had kidnapped locked in one of the hangars at the private airport. Special Agent Metcalf of the FBI is on his way there. You may want to update Sanchez."

"I will." The cop made a clicking sound with his teeth. "You've been busy, Mason. Maybe we need you down here."

Colt grimaced. He didn't know where he belonged, but he had to finish this case first. "Rice still has Petey Stover, and there's an ocean of possibilities where he could take him."

The cop's expression confirmed his worst fears. Working in Miami he'd obviously grown accustomed to losing perps and victims to the waterways.

But Colt was not.

He wouldn't stop or give up until he found Serena's son.

SERENA CRADLED the little girls to her, her heart throbbing at the fear in their eyes. Homer had been so distraught when she'd brought the girls inside and explained where she'd found them that she'd feared he was going to have a heart attack.

She'd managed to calm him, and then he'd bought water and snacks from the vending machines for the children.

"Don't worry, girls," Serena whispered softly. "The police are coming and they're calling your parents and arranging for you to go home."

She wanted to ask details of what Rice and his accomplice had done to them, but fear and the realization that the girls needed loving care, not to be interrogated, kept her from pushing them for information.

Kinsey wiped at her eyes. "The big man was mean," she said in a strained voice. "But the one with the bushy hair was even meaner. He tooked my blanket away."

"And he stoled my doll," Ellie said.

"Petey yelled at him to take us home, but he said we was never gonna see our mamas and daddies again, that they didn't want us anymore." Kinsey gulped back more tears.

Anger mushroomed inside Serena. "Those men lied to you, honey. Your mamas and daddies didn't say that. They've been really upset and looking for you ever since you disappeared, just like I have for Petey."

The screech of a police car interrupted their conversation, and Homer hobbled toward the front to let them in.

Serena glanced up as a dark-haired man in a suit strode in. He stopped in front of her, took one look at the girls and a relieved smile stretched across his face.

"I'm Special Agent Metcalf," he said, giving her a quick nod. Then he knelt in front of the girls. "Kinsey, Ellie, I've already phoned your parents. They're thrilled to know that you're safe and can't wait to see you. They're catching the first available flights to Miami." He lowered his voice to a soothing tone. "Until then we're going to take you to the hospital and make sure you're safe."

Ellie clutched Serena's hand. "I don't like hospitals."

Kinsey's lower lip quivered. "Me neither. They give you shots."

"Shots hurt," Ellie whispered.

The agent looked at Serena as if he was at a loss, and she cuddled both girls to her. "They're not going to give you shots, honey. They just want to make sure the bad men didn't hurt you."

"What if they come back?" Kinsey cried.

"They will never hurt you again," Agent Metcalf said firmly. "I promise you they're going to jail."

Ellie angled her cherub face toward Serena, shivering against her. "Will you go with us?" Ellie whispered.

Serena wanted to be on the streets searching for Petey, but she had to wait on Colt. And there was no way she could abandon these two little girls now.

As SOON AS COLT was allowed to leave the scene of James Ladden's accident, he rushed back to the private airport to meet Serena. When he walked into the terminal, his gaze latched on to her where she sat cradling two tiny little girls. They looked terrified, lost and dirty, and so small and fragile that anger heated his blood. The idea of Rice and Ladden locking them in that hot hangar where they could have died made him want to inflict the same punishment on them.

Although Ladden was dead, Rice wasn't. He'd have his chance....

The sound of an ambulance's wail echoed from outside, and he glanced at Homer, who looked shaken by the ordeal, and then a suited man who he immediately assumed was the fed.

The agent stepped up to introduce himself. "Special Agent Mitchell Metcalf. I hear you're tracking a child kidnapping ring."

"Yeah, but my first priority is finding Petey Stover."

"Right. I've already contacted these girls' parents and they're meeting us at the hospital."

"I promised the girls I'd go with them," Serena said.

Admiration stirred in Colt's chest. Serena was terrified for her son, but still unselfish and loving enough to care for these other children.

The paramedics rushed in and Homer waved them over.

"I'll follow in the rental car," Colt said to Serena. "Then we'll regroup."

Serena soothed the girls while the medics carried them to the ambulance, and they allowed her to climb in the back and ride with them. He and Agent Metcalf followed.

When they arrived at the hospital, Colt was surprised they allowed Serena to stay with the girls, but one of the head nurses took charge, realized the trauma the girls had suffered and insisted they have an adult present who they felt safe with.

Colt and Metcalf drank bad coffee in the waiting room for the next hour and a half while a child psychologist interviewed the girls. Within minutes of one another the girls' parents arrived.

"Where's Kinsey?" Mrs. Jones asked. "Was she hurt?"

The Pinkertons rushed up to them. "And Ellie? Is she all right?"

"Both girls are fine," Agent Metcalf said calmly, then introduced Colt. "Detective Mason and his client Serena Stover traced one of the kidnappers to a private airport. Ms. Stover actually rescued the girls from one of the hangars."

"We want to see our girls," Mr. Pinkerton demanded.

"Yes, please…" Kinsey's mother's voice warbled. "I've been so worried. I thought…"

She didn't finish the sentence. Instead she burst into tears when Serena and the psychologist appeared with Kinsey and Ellie. Both parents rushed to embrace the children, crying and sobbing.

Emotions thickened Colt's throat at the reunion. Relief for the children who'd been found.

Worry for Serena's son who was still lost.

SERENA'S CHEST CONSTRICTED as she watched the girls collapse into their mothers' waiting arms. Kinsey's mother and Ellie's mother and father were all crying, clinging to each other as if they were afraid to let go for fear they would disappear again.

She understood their fears.

Colt slid his arm around her shoulder, pulling her against him. "You did a wonderful thing today, Serena. You're a brave woman."

She dabbed at her eyes. "I don't understand why he left the girls but took Petey."

"Did they say anything about Rice or Ladden?" Colt lowered his voice so the parents couldn't hear. "About what happened to them? Were they hurt?"

She shook her head no. "Thank God. The doctor said there was no evidence of physical or sexual abuse. Except for being emotionally traumatized and slightly dehydrated, the girls are fine."

"I'm sure their parents will get them the counseling they need." Colt paused. "Did either one of them mention where they were held or where Rice was going?'"

Serena's throat hurt. "No. Once the girls are calmer and settled down, a forensic interviewer will talk to them. They might tell us more then, but they claimed that most of the time they were kept in the back of that van. It was dark. They couldn't see anything, and couldn't hear what the men were saying."

Kinsey's mother picked her daughter up and strode toward Serena. "You're the woman who found my little girl, aren't you?"

Serena nodded, and stroked Kinsey's damp hair from her cheek. "I'm glad she's all right."

Ellie's parents joined her with Ellie. "We don't know how to thank you," Ellie's mother said in a shaky voice. Ellie's father hugged his daughter tighter. "You gave us our daughter back. How can we repay you?"

Serena forced a smile. "Just pray that we find my son."

All three parents gave her a collective hug and for a moment Serena nearly broke down.

"It's time for us to go," Colt said after a few minutes.

She wiped her eyes and said goodbye, then lapsed into silence as Colt drove away from the hospital. The traffic and lights of Miami became a blur, the memory of finding those children trapped in that hot building haunting her.

Rice had left the girls. So why hadn't he left Petey there, as well?

She didn't like the answers that came to her.

Colt pulled into a motel off 95 and Serena frowned. "What are you doing?"

"Getting us a room. You haven't slept in days and neither have I. The FBI and police are on the case, the port authorities and airports are on alert, and we both need some rest. We'll start again in a few hours."

"I can't sleep," Serena said.

Colt took her hand. "Then you'll lie down or grab a

shower and rest. Maybe by then we'll get another lead. Right now we don't even know where to search."

Serena knew he was right, but she couldn't stand to sit idly. Her body was too tense, too…exhausted.

Colt parked in front of the motel and she waited inside the car while he secured a room. A minute later, he returned with a key, and drove to the end of the parking lot. Exhausted, she climbed out and went to retrieve her luggage, but he grabbed both their bags and gestured for her to go to the door. For a fraction of a second, she considered arguing over the fact that he'd only rented one room, but she didn't have the energy.

Besides, she didn't want to be alone. Not with her fears and her emotions.

He dumped their bags on the floor, and she opened hers and dragged out a nightshirt then went straight to the shower.

But as she stripped and climbed beneath the water, her emotions overcame her and she finally released more tears of frustration and terror. She wanted to scream and shout and pound the walls. She wanted to find Rice and kill him.

She wanted to hold her son so badly that she felt as if she was going to crack in two. She would never be whole without him.

And she would never stop looking. Not even if she had to travel from country to country combing the streets to find him.

The water turned cold so she towel dried her hair and body and slipped on the satin shirt. When she opened the door, steam billowed out, and she saw Colt lying on the bed with his arms crossed behind his head.

The TV was on, a special news broadcast airing the story about the rescue of the two girls as their parents rushed them to a waiting FBI car to be driven to a local hotel for the night.

Serena's eyes welled with tears again, then she glanced at Colt and something raw inside her snapped.

He was still fully dressed, but the heat and emotions in his eyes sent a deep longing through her. She wanted to be held tonight. To be stroked and soothed and comforted, and loved.

Even if it was only for a few minutes.

Anything to forget the images of those terrified children locked in that hangar.

Anything to stifle the pain of her son's cries when he'd phoned.

Colt's dark gaze caught hers, then flickered with understanding.

She couldn't put her needs above her son, but right now, she had to do whatever she could to survive the pain so she could regain her strength and find him.

Colt held out a hand and she went to him.

Chapter Fifteen

WARNING: SEX AHEAD
SKIP TO PAGE 193

Colt told himself to back off. To tell Serena that they shouldn't make love, but the yearning in her eyes made his protests die in his throat. She had been through an emotional wringer and needed to feel alive.

How many times had he felt that way himself?

Too many to count.

She curled her fingers into his hair, then lowered her mouth to his, and pure hunger heated his blood. She wanted to forget tonight. To drown out the pain and fear eating her alive.

He wanted to give her that reprieve. But not as much as he wanted her for himself.

He had wanted her from the first moment he'd looked into those dazzling troubled eyes. She had secrets, a past she didn't want to share.

But so did he.

She closed her lips over his, and he hungrily consumed her mouth, eagerly pulling her against him. He hadn't been with a woman in ages, hadn't even wanted to. The ones he'd come into contact with on the job weren't worth the trouble. Besides, most of them had lost their morals to the streets.

Not Serena. She had survived the streets and come out a better person for it.

She was everything a man desired. Beautiful. Smart. Tough.

A woman who treasured her family and fought for it.

She rubbed her body against him, and his sex hardened, straining against the fly of his jeans and begging to be inside her.

He stroked her back, trailed his hand down to cup her bottom and pure raw desire surged through him.

But one last seed of rational thought assaulted him, and he flipped her to her back, then paused above her. "Serena," he said roughly. "I don't want to take advantage of you."

"You sound like a broken record," she said with a predatory gleam in her eyes. "Do you want me or not?"

He shoved her legs apart with his knee and settled himself between her thighs. "Of course I want you, but—"

"Shut up," she murmured as she traced her tongue over his lips. "Now make love to me."

He liked a woman who knew what she wanted, asked for what she wanted, a woman who was confident enough to give and take, and Serena was all that and more.

She tore at the buttons on his shirt, and he stripped her nightshirt, his heart hammering as he feasted on her bare breasts, two beautiful golden globes with nipples that stiffened at his perusal, teasing him and inviting him to suckle them into his mouth.

He deepened the kiss, ravaging her sweet taste. Adrenaline, heat and passion ignited between them in a fiery pitch. She stroked his bare chest, moaning as he licked his way down her throat to her breasts, and bit at one turgid nipple.

Arching below him, she offered herself to him with such a throaty moan that he didn't think he'd last much longer.

Smiling as she realized his excitement, she rubbed her crotch against him and licked his ear, and he feasted on her naked body with his eyes. Beauty didn't begin to describe her.

She had scars, too. A jagged one on her thigh that looked like a knife wound, another just below her left breast. For a moment, he saw the vulnerability in her eyes, but he simply lowered his head and kissed the scars, knowing they'd made her the person she was just as his own had shaped him.

Eagerly, she tugged at his jeans, and he stood and shucked them off, grabbing a condom from his pocket before he sank back onto the mattress and allowed her to push his boxers off. Together they rolled on the condom, his bulging erection throbbing painfully in her hands.

Their gazes locked. Raw heat swirled in her expression. Her breathing was erratic. His was choppy, filled with tension as he fought to maintain control and make their lovemaking last.

Naked they lay together, stroking, rubbing, kissing, petting, teasing, entwined, his hard body against her soft, his need pulsing between her thighs, until he could stand it no longer. He rose above her, braced himself on his hands and stroked the silky skin of her inner thighs with his shaft.

She closed her eyes and released a moan that moved him deep within his heart. She wanted him. He wanted to be inside her. To pleasure her and make her his.

Hell, he was falling in love with her.

The idea sent a streak of terror through him, but she gripped his hips and pulled him toward her, and he thrust inside her. The first feel of her heat enclosing him, sucking at his length, milking him with her femininity, made his body quake.

She wrapped her legs around him as he inched from her sweetness, then slid back inside, pounding deeper. A low groan erupted from deep within her and she clung to him, her whisper of need begging for fulfillment.

He pumped harder and faster, thrusting deeper each time, stroking her inner chamber with his fullness, building a rhythm that quickly spiraled out of control, leaving them both panting and sweating and shouting as her orgasm rocked through her. At her outburst, he finally allowed himself to taste the sweet bliss of his own release.

And when he came inside her, and she nuzzled her head into his chest, clinging to him, his chest clenched with love and fear.

He knew she'd been seeking comfort tonight. That

when she had her son back, she'd move on and he would have to as, well.

But he didn't know how the hell he was going to let her go.

OK IT's SAFE NOW!

SERENA'S BODY QUIVERED in the aftermath of their love-making and she huddled in Colt's arms, savoring his masculine scent and the strength of his big hard body. For just a moment, she allowed herself to forget the nightmare that had become her life.

But Petey's little voice interrupted, his cries for her echoing in her head. She'd had a lousy childhood and had wanted to protect him from anything bad. But she'd failed.

Colt traced a finger over a scar on her shoulder, and she tensed, remembering the foster father who had given her that wound. The physical ones had healed but the mental ones remained, rising to haunt her in the darkness.

She thought Parker had understood, yet they had never really talked about it because she'd kept that part of her hidden, afraid he'd see her differently if he knew the truth. That he'd see her as unlovable and would realize why her parents hadn't wanted her.

"Thank you, Colt," she whispered.

He cupped her face between his hands. "You don't have to thank me. I wanted you, Serena. Maybe it's wrong but I still do."

Serena shook her head in denial. "You wouldn't say that if you knew the real me."

Colt started to say something, but his cell phone

buzzed, and he reached for it and connected the call. "Colt Mason." A pause. "Yes." Another pause, then Colt sat up and grabbed his clothes off the floor. "Hang on, I'll be right there."

Ending the call, he vaulted off the bed to dress.

"What is it, Colt?" Serena asked.

"That was Dasha. She was scared. She's in Miami and has information about the kidnapping ring. She wants us to meet her at the docks."

Serena's heart careened into double time. "Oh, God. She might know where Petey is." She jumped off the bed and scrambled to find her jeans and shirt.

Within seconds, they were both dressed and rushing out the door. Colt tucked his gun inside his pants, unlocked the rental car, and they raced toward the docks. The late night crowd was still out partying on the main drag, but as they left the center of town, traffic thinned and the waterway stretched before them.

Houseboats, sailboats and speedboats popped into view and at the far end, a series of storage buildings butted up to the docks. The ocean rippled, waves crashing the shore, the sound of a motor puttering in the distance breaking the silence.

Colt pulled into the parking lot, and Serena searched the darkness, the dimly lit boat ramps, the storage area, looking for signs of Dasha or Rice.

"Stay alert," Colt warned as they climbed out. "This could be a setup."

Serena nodded. He didn't have to tell her the dangers of the street. Not that they would stop her from going after her son. Nothing would.

Together they walked up the dock, glancing from one boat to the next. Partiers on a houseboat were drinking and dancing to loud music, two fishermen burned a low light as they coasted out to sea, and a shrimp boat glowed in the distance.

Across the inlet was another set of docks. Colt spotted a lone figure staggering in the dark near a storage container. "Over there. It's Dasha. She's hurt."

Colt pointed toward the lower ramp and ran toward it. Serena followed, staying close behind him as they jogged toward the figure. The scent of salt water blended with the strong odor of fish and shrimp, the balmy heat of the night making her feel clammy all over.

She shoved her hair from her face, squinting through the darkness as she spotted Dasha stagger between two buildings. A shot rang out, pinging above their heads, and Colt drew his gun.

"Stay down!"

Serena crouched lower and veered into the alley. Colt halted at the corner, firing back at the shooter, and she ran on, her stomach knotting when she saw Dasha collapse onto the ground.

She hurried to Dasha, knelt and touched the woman's shoulder. "Dasha?"

Dasha groaned, and Serena turned her body over, gasping at the sight of blood seeping through her fingers where she held them over her abdomen.

"Dasha, it's Serena. Who shot you?"

"A man, works for Rice," Dasha whispered hoarsely. "I followed him…wanted to find your son. But he found out I talked to you…" Her voice broke, perspiration beading on her face and neck. "One of his men brought me here to Rice."

Serena ripped off the bottom portion of her T-shirt, folded it up and pressed it on Dasha's wound. "Keep pressure on it. I'll call an ambulance."

Dasha caught her hand before she could move. "Wait. Don't go."

"I'm just going to get help."

"No, first, your son…he's here…"

"Where? Is he all right?"

Dasha moaned, her pallor pasty white, then lifted a bloody finger and gestured toward the right. "He's in the boat on the end. Rice…was going to leave with him tonight. You have to hurry…"

Serena gripped Dasha's hand. "Thanks."

"Just go get your son," Dasha whispered.

Serena nodded, then stood and glanced to the side in search of Colt. More shots echoed in the night, and she prayed Colt didn't get hit as she ran toward the boat.

She paused before she boarded, scanning the upper level for Rice or one of his cronies, but saw no one. She hesitated, contemplating going back for Colt, but another gunshot blasted the air, and she jumped onto the deck. For all she knew, the man who'd shot Dasha was trying to fend them off so Rice could escape.

She didn't intend to let that happen.

Frantic, she searched the main deck, then tiptoed down the stairs, listening for any sound to indicate Rice was on board setting a trap. But only the sound of the water lapping against the boat danced around her.

She glanced around the main cabin, but it was empty.

Then a noise penetrated the quiet. A small tapping sound.

Her heart began to race. It was coming from one of the smaller cabins down the hall.

She hurried toward the noise, cautiously checking the first two cabins, but found them empty. Then another sound broke the silence.

A soft cry.

Petey?

Dear God. Her heart sputtered as she rushed to the cabin and jiggled the door. Dammit, it was locked.

"Petey?"

A muffled sound followed, then more thumping and the sound of a whistle.

"Hang on, honey. Let me find something to open the door." Adrenaline surged through her, and she raced back to the main cabin in search of a key. She rummaged through the drawers, the desk, then checked the wall for a key ring but didn't find one.

Rice must have taken it with him.

Memories of her street life resurfaced, and she rushed to the desk drawer and searched for a paper clip. She found one in the top drawer, bent it to use as a tool, then ran back to the locked door and jammed it in the lock.

Inside, the crying and pounding grew louder.

"I'm coming, honey, hang on." Two more tries, and the lock clicked. Breathing deeply, she shoved open the door and spotted her son curled on the tiny bed in the corner with his hands and feet tied, his mouth gagged. Somehow he'd managed to slip the end of the whistle beneath the gag just enough to blow it.

Pure rage mingled with relief, and she rushed to him. Fear darkened Petey's eyes, but she saw his relief, as well, and lowered herself on the bed beside him.

Her hands shook as she untied his hands and feet, and removed the gag. Tears streaked his little face, and he looked tired and frightened, but he seemed unharmed.

"Mommy!" Petey cried. "I knew you'd find me."

Emotions clogged her throat as he threw his arms around her neck. Serena wrapped her arms around him and held him, tears flowing as she rocked him against her.

But they couldn't stay here long. Rice would come back.

And when he did, he would kill her to get to Petey.

Chapter Sixteen

Colt hit Rice's crony with the third bullet he fired. The man dropped like a rock, blood spurting from his chest. Colt checked the alley for Rice, but didn't see him so he walked over to the beefy gunman and checked for a pulse.

Nothing.

He retrieved the man's weapon, tucked it into the back of his jeans then headed toward the alley where Serena had chased Dasha, checking over his shoulder and the surrounding area. His gut tightened at the sight of Dasha lying on the ground motionless.

He knelt beside her, grimacing at the blood seeping through the rag she held pressed to her stomach. "Dasha?"

She moaned and slowly opened her eyes. Her pupils were dilated, her pallor gray. "Serena...went after Petey."

"Where?"

She pointed a shaky hand toward the boats. "The boat on the end..."

"I'll get help." He punched in 911 and asked for an

ambulance, then raced toward the boat. Just as he neared it, a scream split the air.

Serena.

Dammit.

Adrenaline surged through him, and he sprinted toward the boat. But just as he climbed on board, he spotted Rice dragging Serena from downstairs. The bastard had Serena around the neck in a chokehold. Petey was nowhere in sight.

Fury turned his veins to ice. If he hurt one hair on Serena's head, he'd kill him with his bare hands.

"Let her go, Rice," Colt demanded.

His gaze caught with Serena's and he saw the fear but also trust, and his lungs tightened.

Rice jammed his weapon at Serena's head. "You're not going to stop me now."

"Where's Petey?" Colt asked through gritted teeth.

"He's downstairs," Serena said with a jerk of her head.

Then she'd seen him and he was alive. So now Rice planned to kill Serena and take off with her son.

"Come on, Rice. There's no way you're going to get away with this. Put down the gun so I don't have to kill you."

Rice barked a laugh and jerked Serena's arm. "You shoot and she's dead, too."

Serena was looking at him oddly, a mixture of acceptance and determination. "Don't give in to him, Colt. Just save Petey, that's all that matters."

The hell with that. *She* mattered to him, too. He

didn't intend to sacrifice her life for her son's. He'd save them both.

Colt's hand felt unsteady, but he forced himself to inhale and rely on his training. He had to focus, block out everything but the target.

Rice twisted Serena's arm behind her back, this time so hard she winced. "Put your gun down, Mason, and I'll think about letting her live."

Colt gritted his teeth, raised his hands as if to surrender. But suddenly Serena lifted her arm and jabbed her elbow in Rice's stomach, at the same time stomping on his foot.

Rice was so shocked he momentarily loosened his grip, and Serena dropped to the floor. Colt fired the gun and sent a bullet sailing toward Rice.

But Rice dodged the bullet and lunged at Colt, knocking his gun to the floor. Colt slammed his fist in Rice's nose and bones crunched, blood spurting. Rice grunted and fired his weapon, but Colt threw his body sideways, avoiding the bullet. Then he swung his other hand up, fighting for Rice's gun.

Serena scrambled to her hands and knees, then raced toward the steps to get Petey.

Colt and Rice fought and struggled, pounding each other, but Colt was stronger than the bastard, and finally managed to pin him against the rail.

"You framed Serena and kidnapped her son. Who were you going to sell him to, Rice?"

Rice spat at him. "It was her husband's fault. He tried to shut down my business."

Serena's arrest, the kidnapping, the vile idea that Rice

would sell children, the torment Serena and Petey had endured taunted Colt, and he punched Rice over and over until his face was a bloody mess, and the man sagged against him.

Sirens wailed in the distance, then he heard Serena's voice calling his name as emergency lights twirled in the darkness.

Still his rage was so intense, he wanted to make Rice suffer more. Wanted to kill him then toss him into the ocean for the sharks to feed upon.

But Serena and Petey moved closer, and he caught Petey's terrified look. Sickened by his own rage, Colt released the man. Rice fell to the floor with a thump.

A minute later, police and medics rushed onto the boat.

"That man kidnapped my son," Serena cried. "And he tried to kill me."

Colt identified himself, pointed out Dasha's location, then watched as the local officer handcuffed Rice.

Rice opened his eyes as the medics loaded him onto a stretcher. "You think you won, but you're wrong," Rice growled.

Colt grabbed him by the throat, uncaring that the officer was watching. "What are you talking about?"

"The kidnapping ring, I'm only a small peon," Rice snarled. "The head honcho will have your head for interfering with his shipment."

Colt shook Rice. "Who is the head of the business?"

Rice spit blood at him. "I'm not a snitch."

"No, just a coward. You prey on kids and now you're too scared your boss will kill you if you talk."

Rice merely smiled through the blood on his face then turned to the police officer. "I want a lawyer."

Colt balled his hands into fists. Damn Rice. If the cops weren't present, he'd beat the man until he talked. Instead he had to watch as they carted him off, leaving Colt with more questions.

Serena was holding Petey, the two of them clinging to one another, emotional but safe.

He had done his job. Petey was safe with his mother.

His heart gave a pang. He wanted to be part of that unit, to go home with them and keep them safe forever.

But there were other kids in danger from this kidnapping ring. Other kids like Petey who needed his help.

And he couldn't close the case until the leader was caught and the kidnapping ring disbanded.

SERENA HELD PETEY close as she answered the police officer's questions, and Colt filled the police in on everything they'd learned.

She carried Petey with her to say goodbye to Dasha as they loaded her into the ambulance. Dasha was weak, but the medics had started an IV and assured Serena the young woman would live.

Dasha looked up at her as she approached, her expression when she saw Serena holding her son tugging at Serena's heart. "Thank you so much for calling. You saved my son's life."

A tear trickled down Dasha's ashen face. "Parker died trying to stop this from happening. I couldn't let Rice get away with it."

"You loved my husband," Serena said.

Dasha started to protest, but Serena gripped her hand. "It's all right. I understand."

An odd look filled Dasha's eyes, and Serena realized that this young woman was more like her than she would ever have thought. She had been dealt some hard knocks and was trying to survive. But in the end, she'd done the right thing.

Maybe Parker had seen those same characteristics in Dasha that he'd seen in her and had been trying to save her, as well.

"If you ever need anything, Dasha, call me," Serena said and meant it.

The young woman squeezed her hand. "I'm getting out of the business," she said, although her voice sounded unsure. "I always wanted to do hair."

Serena smiled. "Then go for it. I'll be your first client."

When she turned, Colt was watching her, his expression a mask. But something had shifted between them. She'd thought she'd sensed an emotional connection between them when they'd made love.

But now she felt him pulling away.

He smiled at Petey. "How're you doing, buddy?"

Petey lifted his chin. "Better now you and Mommy found me." He held up the whistle. "It worked. I blowed it and Mommy found me."

"Good. Did that man hurt you?"

Petey shook his head. "But he scared me, and he tried to hurt Mommy... He won't come back?"

Serena hugged him tighter. "No, baby, he's going to jail."

Petey turned to Colt. "Mr. Colt, is that right?"

"Yes," Colt said. "Now come on, there's a flight waiting for us to take you home."

Serena carried Petey to the car, and Colt drove them to the airport. Her son fell asleep on the plane, his head in Serena's lap, and she finally closed her eyes and allowed herself to rest.

Hours later, after a plane switch in Atlanta, then another plane ride to Asheville, Colt drove them back to Sanctuary. She and Petey had slept most of the trip, the exhaustion finally catching up with her.

When they arrived at her house, Colt insisted on carrying Petey inside and to his room. Serena helped him into his pj's, tucked his beloved giant panda in with him and kissed him good-night.

She wanted to talk to Colt, but when she returned to the den, he was standing by the door ready to go. His expression remained stoic, pensive almost.

Final, as if he was going to say goodbye and she would never see him again.

"Thank you for all you've done," Serena said. "I... couldn't have survived this ordeal without you. You gave me back my son."

"I'm just glad Petey is safe." Colt tensed, his shoulder blades rigid. "But I have to follow up, find out who's behind the kidnapping ring."

She stared at him for a long moment, knowing she

couldn't argue or change this man. He was too honorable. Just like Parker, finding the truth, attaining justice for the innocent, it was in their blood.

She wanted to tell him it was all right. But she'd vowed never to get involved with another man who chose a dangerous job over his family. And Petey wasn't even Colt's son. How could she expect him to change? To choose them?

She saw it in his eyes anyway. He had already made his choice. He was erecting walls. Walls she understood.

She had thrown up walls all her life.

What was one more time?

She and Petey were a family. When Colt left, nothing would change that.

Like Colt had said, she had survived the past. She had survived losing Parker.

She would survive again.

Chapter Seventeen

Four months later

Serena smiled at Madelyn Andrews Walker and accepted a cookie from the tray Brianna offered her. After she had returned home safely with Petey, the other wives of the GAI detectives had befriended her.

Petey adored baby Ryan, liked Rebecca, Nina's little girl, and Ruby, Leah's daughter, but he especially enjoyed playing with Madelyn's twin girls, Sara and Cissy. Serena would always have a special place in her heart for Cissy herself. After all, the little girl had saved her son's life.

Leah held her newborn son in her arms, cradling him close, and Ruby walked over to plant a kiss on her brother's forehead.

"He's a good baby," Leah said softly, her proud smile beaming.

"Yep, he pees and poops and sleeps and cries just like he's s'posed to," Ruby chirped. "But I'll be glad when he gets bigger and can play like Petey. Even Ryan can do more stuff."

She plopped down beside the toddler, then tried to teach him how to stack the plastic blocks.

Serena treasured her new friends and felt as if they'd become a family to her and Petey.

The only thing missing was Colt.

He'd been undercover for four months now with no word, and she worried every day that he wouldn't return.

The phone trilled, and Leah reached for it. "Hello." Pause. "Oh, gosh, that's good news. Yes, we'll turn on the TV now."

Leah disconnected and started to rise to retrieve the remote, but Nina waved her off. "Let me get it. What's going on?"

Leah smiled her thanks. "Gage said Colt finally managed to catch and disband the kidnapping ring. There's a special news coverage airing now."

Nina punched the on button. Seconds later, the news story flashed onto the screen.

"Folks, we're coming to you live from Miami. Just moments ago, police reported that they have arrested the major players behind an international child kidnapping ring." Cameras panned an estate on one of the remote islands off the coast.

"FBI Special Agent Metcalf said he's been working with a team of federal agents, local law officers and a private detective from GAI in North Carolina on this case for months."

Serena's heart pounded. "Where's Colt?"

Petey ran up and leaned into her. "Mommy, is Mr. Colt there?"

On the screen, sirens twirled and blinked in the darkness, dozens of police officers scurried about, three men in suits were being hauled to police cars in handcuffs, and another man lay on the ground soaked in blood.

Serena knotted her hands. "Colt?"

"In what came as a surprise, a former law officer from Raleigh's police department, Geoff Harbison, was helping the feds. Reports indicate that he had been coerced into revealing the whereabouts of another law officer, Parker Stover, who was killed two years ago when he began investigating the ring. Harbison recently turned state's evidence in order to arrest the leader behind the organization. Ricco DelGaldo is in custody, although his bodyguard was killed during the takedown tonight."

"Thank God they finally caught him," Madelyn said.

Leah made a sound of disgust. "I hope he rots in jail."

Ryan started fussing so Brianna picked him up and propped him on her hip. "Where's Colt?"

Serena hugged Petey to her. Yes, where was he?

An ambulance screeched up, and she watched as two medics jogged around the house to the back and returned moments later carrying a man on the stretcher. Her breath hissed between her teeth when she saw the black hair, that chiseled face. Colt.

"Oh, no, Colt's hurt," Leah gasped.

Petey clenched Serena's arm. "Mommy…"

Serena cradled her son next to her, studying Colt. He was unconscious, blood soaked his shirt and pants, and she couldn't tell if he was breathing.

"He has to be all right," she whispered.

The camera panned back to the news reporter. "Unfortunately GAI Detective Colt Mason, the detective who spearheaded the investigation, was also shot. He is being airlifted to Miami Dade Hospital for emergency surgery."

Serena's heart was breaking. She'd missed Colt so much the past few months, had feared for his life. She'd drawn on that fear as a reminder that they didn't belong together. That she didn't want Petey raised in an environment perpetually riddled with worry and fear and uncertainty.

But the look on his face told her that he missed Colt anyway.

Colt was a hero just as Parker had been.

And she was in love with the man.

"I have to go to him," Serena said. "I have to see him."

Petey tugged at her arm again. "I wanna go, too, Mommy."

Brianna scooted onto the couch beside Petey. "Sweetheart, I don't think they'll let you in the hospital."

Serena glanced at her new friends, desperate. She didn't know what to do, only that she had to tell Colt that she loved him, that she wanted him in her life.

"Go to him," Leah urged softly.

Madelyn patted her shoulder. "Petey can stay with us and the girls. He'll be all right."

Serena stared at them for a moment, then hugged her son. They were right. Colt had risked his life for her and

Petey and for all the innocent children who had been victimized.

She had to make sure he knew how she felt.

COLT FELT WEAK, but mostly irritated. He hated hospitals.

At least he'd caught the leader behind the kidnapping ring. The last four months he'd immersed himself in the dark underbelly of human trafficking, and at times he'd nearly lost his control.

He opened his palm where he held the photo of Petey and Serena and stared at it as he had so many times over the past few months. But their faces had helped him find his way back.

The end justified the means.

That was part of detective work he'd accepted long ago. So many nights he'd lain awake struggling, afraid his fury over the injustice of what they were doing would eat him alive.

But one look at the kids and he'd realized that he was not like the cold, heartless men and women who preyed on the young and helpless.

He pressed a hand to the bandage on his chest and tried to sit up. The shooter had barely missed his heart. An inch closer and he'd be dead.

But the pain in his chest had more to do with the longing and hollow feeling that had dogged him ever since he'd left Sanctuary. He would go back there as soon as he was healed. Back to his empty house.

Back to being alone.

Dammit, he'd always liked his privacy. The quiet. Having a house to himself.

But the thought of it now made his chest hurt even more.

The *beep beep* of the monitors in the room echoed, reminding him that he was weak now and couldn't go after Serena yet, even if he wanted to.

Did he want to?

Yes.

But did she still love her dead husband?

Exhaustion weighed on him, and he finally succumbed to the drugs and pain, closed his eyes and let sleep claim him. Nightmares of finding a group of terrified children being traded for money, sold for sex and slavery, haunted him.

Sometime later, the sound of the door opening jarred him awake, and he opened his eyes. For a moment, he thought he was still dreaming or that the drugs were causing him to hallucinate. Except this was no nightmare, it was his fantasy.

Serena stood in the doorway wearing a white sundress, her russet hair flowing around her shoulders, her face angelic in the dim light of the room. He blinked to make sure he wasn't imagining her.

"Colt?"

He blinked again, then pushed himself up to a sitting position, but the stitches in his chest pulled and he winced.

"Don't move and hurt yourself." Serena crossed the room, grabbed a pillow and tucked it behind his head, then helped him ease himself into a more comfortable position.

"What are you doing here?" Colt asked.

"I saw the news," Serena said, her eyes roving over him with concern, and other emotions he couldn't identify. "They were carrying you on a stretcher..."

"I'm fine," he said forcing a bland expression when the pain in his body was throbbing relentlessly. "Doctors patched me up. I'll be home in no time."

Serena dragged the corner chair next to his bed and covered his hand with hers. "You're a hero, Colt. You arrested the guy behind the kidnapping ring and saved no telling how many children and families from suffering..."

Colt swallowed. He didn't want to discuss the case and what he'd had to do to catch the bastard. Or the horrible things he'd witnessed.

"How's Petey?" Colt asked.

A smile filled Serena's eyes. "He's great. I...was afraid he'd be traumatized, and we met with a counselor, but he seems to have bounced back. The wives of all the GAI agents banded together and gave us support." She paused. "Petey really likes the other children, especially the Andrews' twins."

Colt smiled. "Kids are more resilient than we think."

Serena nodded. "He asks about you all the time." Her smile faded. "He wanted to come, but I didn't think they'd let him in the hospital."

"I'd like to see him when I get back," Colt said and wanted to say more but hesitated. "I need to return his piggy bank."

"Of course." Serena glanced away, then cleared her throat. "What about the other money, the cash in the duffel bag?"

"I mentioned it to Detective Shaw. He said he found no record of missing cash for the department. It's yours."

Serena blinked in shock, then smiled. "I'm going to donate it to Magnolia Manor."

Admiration stirred inside Colt. Of course, Serena would do something unselfish with it. That was only one of the qualities he loved about her.

Serena shifted, suddenly anxious. Nervous. "Well, I just wanted to see if you were okay."

"I am." He didn't know what to do or say, except that he loved her and he wanted her to be happy. But he couldn't ask for her love or to be part of her family. He couldn't replace her husband.

So he had to put aside his own needs.

She stood and walked to the door, then paused there and looked back at him. He memorized her face, her delicate features, and clutched the photo in his hand tighter. He didn't want to let it go just as he didn't want to let her go.

"I'll see you back in Sanctuary," Serena said softly. "Stop by and visit Petey whenever you want. He'd like that."

His heart sank. Petey would like it. But what about Serena?

SERENA'S NERVES PINGED back and forth as she walked out the door. God help her, she'd come here to confess her love to Colt, but she'd frozen. What if he didn't return her feelings?

Coward.

Disgusted with herself, she twisted her hands together. She had faced trouble on the streets without hesitating, but admitting she loved Colt immobilized her.

Geoff suddenly appeared from the waiting area, his arm in a sling. "Can we talk for a minute? Please."

She nodded and stepped into the corner with him. "I saw the news, Geoff. What you did."

"I'm so sorry, Serena." He dropped his head forward, his voice tortured. "I know it doesn't change things, that it's my fault Parker was killed, but I honestly didn't know they were going to kill him."

Tears laced his voice, his remorse a palpable force, and Serena remembered his wife had been ill and his handicapped son needed therapy. He'd been desperate, and had done everything he could to protect his family.

How could she blame him for that when she understood that kind of desperation and fear, that kind of love?

She gently touched his arm. "I understand, Geoff. I…I know what it's like to love your family so much you'd do anything for them."

"But Parker's death…it's my fault." His voice choked. "And I can't bring him back."

"No…" Serena said softly, then pulled him into a hug. "You didn't kill him, Geoff. We both know the job…it was dangerous."

Geoff wiped at his eyes and looked up at her. "I don't know how you can ever forgive me."

Serena squeezed his arm. "Parker wouldn't want me to hate you. He'd want you to forgive yourself and be there for your son."

Geoff straightened but he still looked tormented. "Your fellow...Mason," Geoff said gruffly. "He's a stand-up man, Serena. He went undercover for you and Petey. He carried a photo of you two in his wallet and I saw him looking at it all the time."

Serena frowned. He had a photo of her and Petey with him? He must have taken it from her house. "He was just doing his job, Geoff."

"No. He cares about you. He's just the kind of man who doesn't use flowery words. Instead, he shows you by his actions."

And he'd finished this case because of her and her son.

So why had she been such a coward?

She refused to be one again.

"Take care, Geoff. I have to talk to Colt." She whirled around and hurried back to his room. When she opened the door, Colt was standing at the doorway, clutching his chest, his dark eyes determined.

Surprise lit his face when he saw her, then a sheepish grin. "I was coming to see you," he said. "To stop you from leaving."

"You were?"

He nodded, unfolded his hand and showed her the photograph. "I missed you," he said gruffly. He pressed the picture over his heart. "But I kept this close to me so I would always know that you and Petey were near me."

Serena's heart completely melted. "I love you," Serena whispered. "I...was too afraid to tell you, but I do. I've missed you, and I want you to come back to Sanctuary and be with me and Petey and for us to be a family."

Colt's grin widened. "You do?"

She nodded, the flash of emotion in his eyes touching her deeply. "Yes. That is, if you don't mind a ready-made family."

He slid the picture in his pocket, then cupped her face between his hands. "I love you, too, Serena, and I'll do my damnedest to be a good father to Petey."

He lowered his lips and teased hers with his tongue. "Marry me, Serena."

Tears filled Serena's eyes. "Yes."

Colt made a low sound in his throat, his sultry eyes sparkling with desire and hunger and such love that Serena's reservations disintegrated.

Geoff was right.

She and Colt didn't need words. Instead, she helped him back to bed, then lay down beside him, kissed him passionately, and showed him with her actions just how much she loved him.

* * * * *

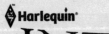
INTRIGUE

COMING NEXT MONTH

Available August 9, 2011

HICNM0711

REQUEST YOUR FREE BOOKS!
2 FREE NOVELS PLUS 2 FREE GIFTS!

Harlequin®

INTRIGUE®

BREATHTAKING ROMANTIC SUSPENSE

Once bitten, twice shy. That's Gabby Wade's motto—
especially when it comes to Adamson men.
And the moment she meets Jon Adamson her theory
is confirmed. But with each encounter a little something
sparks between them, making her wonder if she's been
too hasty to dismiss this one!

Enjoy this sneak peek from ONE GOOD REASON
by Sarah Mayberry, available August 2011
from Harlequin® Superromance®.

Gabby Wade's heartbeat thumped in her ears as she marched to her office. She wanted to pretend it was because of her brisk pace returning from the file room, but she wasn't that good a liar.

Her heart was beating like a tom-tom because Jon Adamson had touched her. In a very male, very possessive way. She could still feel the heat of his big hand burning through the seat of her khakis as he'd steadied her on the ladder.

It had taken every ounce of self-control to tell him to unhand her. What she'd really wanted was to grab him by his shirt and, well, explore all those urges his touch had instantly brought to life.

While she might not like him, she was wise enough to understand that it wasn't always about liking the other person. Sometimes it was about pure animal attraction.

Refusing to think about it, she turned to work. When she'd typed in the wrong figures three times, Gabby admitted she was too tired and too distracted. Time to call it a day.

As she was leaving, she spied Jon at his workbench in the shop. His head was propped on his hand as he studied blueprints. It wasn't until she got closer that she saw his eyes were shut.

He looked oddly boyish. There was something innocent and unguarded in his expression. She felt a weakening in her resistance to him.

"Jon." She put her hand on his shoulder, intending to shake him awake. Instead, it rested there like a caress.

His eyes snapped open.

"You were asleep."

"No, I was, uh, visualizing something on this design." He gestured to the blueprint in front of him then rubbed his eyes.

That gesture dealt a bigger blow to her resistance. She realized it wasn't only animal attraction pulling them together. She took a step backward as if to get away from the knowledge.

She cleared her throat. "I'm heading off now."

He gave her a smile, and she could see his exhaustion.

"Yeah, I should, too." He stood and stretched. The hem of his T-shirt rose as he arched his back and she caught a flash of hard male belly. She looked away, but it was too late. Her mind had committed the image to permanent memory.

And suddenly she knew, for good or bad, she'd never look at Jon the same way again.

Find out what happens next in ONE GOOD REASON, available August 2011 from Harlequin® Superromance®!

Celebrating

Blaze™ **10** *years of*

red-hot reads

Featuring a special August author lineup of
six fan-favorite authors who have written
for Blaze™ from the beginning!

The Original Sexy Six:

Vicki Lewis Thompson
Tori Carrington
Kimberly Raye
Debbi Rawlins
Julie Leto
Jo Leigh

Pick up all six Blaze™
Special Collectors' Edition titles!

August 2011

MYSTERY UNRAVELED
Find the answers to the puzzles in last month's INTRIGUE titles!

Hidden Word
(Writing & Computers)

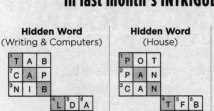

¹T	A	B
²C	A	P
³N	I	B

			⁴L	⁵D	⁶A
			A	E	L
			B	L	T

Hidden Word: TABLET

Hidden Word
(House)

¹P	O	T
²P	A	N
³C	A	N

			⁴T	⁵F	⁶B
			I	R	A
			N	Y	Y

Hidden Word: PANTRY

Figure Counting
(Squares & Rectangles)

Thirty-eight

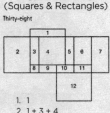

1. 1
2. 1 + 3 + 4

Figure Counting
(Triangles)

Eight

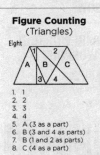

1. 1
2. 2
3. 3
4. 4
5. A (3 as a part)
6. B (3 and 4 as parts)
7. B (1 and 2 as parts)
8. C (4 as a part)

Matchstick Puzzle
(12-Matchstick Arrangement)

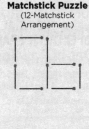

Matchstick Puzzle
(20-Matchstick Arrangement)

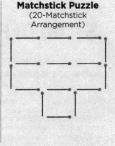

BOOST YOUR BRAIN

Receive **$1.50 off** either

or

Available wherever books are sold!

$1.50 OFF either THE TOTAL BRAIN WORKOUT or EXTREME BRAIN WORKOUT

Offer valid from July 1, 2011, to January 31, 2012.
Redeemable at participating retail outlets. Limit one coupon per purchase.
Valid in the U.S.A. and Canada only.

52609897

5 65373 00078 6   (8100)0 11751